The Husband

Aaron Abilene

Published by Syphon Creative, 2024.

This is a work of fiction. Similarities to real people, places, or events are entirely coincidental.

THE HUSBAND

First edition. November 25, 2024.

Copyright © 2024 Aaron Abilene.

ISBN: 979-8230992462

Written by Aaron Abilene.

Also by Aaron Abilene

505
505
505: Resurrection

Balls
Dead Awake
Before The Dead Awake
Dead Sleep
Bulletproof Balls

Carnival Game
Full Moon Howl
Donovan
Shades of Z

Codename
The Man in The Mini Van

Deadeye
Deadeye & Friends
Cowboys Vs Aliens

Ferris
Life in Prescott
Afterlife in Love
Tragic Heart

Island
Paradise Island
The Lost Island
The Lost Island 2
The Lost Island 3
The Island 2

Pandemic
Pandemic

Prototype
Prototype
The Compound

Slacker
Slacker 2
Slacker 3
Slacker: Dead Man Walkin'

Survivor Files
Survivor Files: Day 1
Survivor Files : Day 1 Part 2
Survivor Files : Day 2
Survivor Files : On The Run
Survivor Files : Day 3
Survivor Files : Day 4
Survivor Files : Day 5
Survivor Files : Day 6
Survivor Files : Day 7
Survivor Files : Day 8
Survivor Files : Day 9
Survivor Files : Day 10
Survivor Files : Day 11
Survivor Files : Day 12
Survivor Files : Day 13
Survivor Files : Day 14
Survivor Files : Day 15
Survivor Files : Day 16
Survivor Files : Day 17
Survivor Files : Day 18
Survivor Files : Day 19
Survivor Files : Day 20

Texas
Devil Child of Texas
A Vampire in Texas

The Author
Breaking Wind
Yellow Snow
Dragon Snatch
Golden Showers
Nether Region
Evil Empire

Thomas
Quarantine
Contagion
Eradication
Isolation
Immune
Pathogen
Bloodline
Decontaminated

TPD
Trailer Park Diaries
Trailer Park Diaries 2
Trailer Park Diaries 3

Virus
Raising Hell

Zombie Bride
Zombie Bride
Zombie Bride 2
Zombie Bride 3

Standalone
The Victims of Pinocchio
A Christmas Nightmare
Pain
Fat Jesus
A Zombie's Revenge
The Headhunter
Crash
Tranq
The Island
Dog
The Quiet Man
Joe Superhero
Feral
Good Guys
Romeo and Juliet and Zombies
The Gamer
Becoming Alpha
Dead West
Small Town Blues

Shades of Z: Redux
The Gift of Death
Killer Claus
Skarred
Home Sweet Home
Alligator Allan
10 Days
Army of The Dumbest Dead
Kid
The Cult of Stupid
9 Time Felon
Slater
Bad Review: Hannah Dies
Me Again
Maurice and Me
The Family Business
Lightning Rider : Better Days
Lazy Boyz
The Sheep
Wild
The Flood
Extinction
Good Intentions
Dark Magic
Sparkles The Vampire Clown
From The Future, Stuck in The Past
Rescue
Knock Knock
Creep
Honest John
Urbex
She's Psycho
Unfinished

Neighbors
Misery, Nevada
Vicious Cycle
Relive
Romeo and Juliet: True Love Conquers All
Dead Road
Florida Man
Hunting Sarah
The Great American Zombie Novel
Carnage
Marge 3 Toes
Random Acts of Stupidity
Born Killer
The Abducted
Whiteboy
Broken Man
Graham Hiney
Bridge
15
Paper Soldiers
Zartan
The Concepts of a Plan
The Firsts in Life
Vlad The Bad
The Husband
Giant Baby

The Husband

Written by Aaron Abilene

Mark Jennings stood in the kitchen, his hand steady as he poured the steaming coffee into a mug. The rich aroma wafted up, enveloping him. He closed his eyes and breathed it in deeply. Fuck, that smells good. A hint of a smile crossed his face as he took that first precious sip, savoring the bold flavor on his tongue.

He drained half the mug in a few long gulps. The hot liquid burned going down but he didn't give a shit. Checking the time, he saw it was just past six AM. Right on schedule. Mark set the mug in the sink with a clink and strode to the garage.

His trusty blue kayak waited for him, paddles crossed neatly on top. All his gear was laid out, prepped and ready to go. He ran a hand along the smooth hull. Today's the day. No more fucking around. Time to do what needs to be done.

With practiced motions, he started loading equipment into the kayak. Dry bags, first aid kit, his lucky pocketknife. Each item had its place. As he worked, his mind churned with dark thoughts barely held in check. But out on the water, things would be different. Clearer. He'd finally quiet the noise in his head. And make the hard choices he'd been avoiding for too damn long.

The garage door creaked open, spilling soft morning light across the concrete floor. Rachel stepped inside, a vision of domestic bliss in her pale blue robe. Her dark hair was still mussed from sleep, but her eyes sparkled as she smiled at him.

"Morning, babe." She sauntered over, bare feet padding on the cool surface. "Getting an early start, I see."

Mark straightened, his lips quirking. "No rest for the wicked, you know how it is." He pulled her close, hands drifting low on her hips. She smelled like lavender and clean linen.

Rachel laughed, the sound bright in the quiet garage. "Mmm, and you're the wickedest of them all, aren't you?" Her fingers played with the hair at the nape of his neck, sending little shivers down his spine.

"Damn straight." He nipped playfully at her earlobe. "Someone's gotta keep this town in line."

She swatted his chest. "My hero." Rolling her eyes, but he could see the fondness underneath. "Just try not to piss off any more locals today, alright? I'd like my man back in one piece."

"No promises." Mark winked roguishly. "You know trouble always seems to find me."

"Ain't that the truth." Rachel shook her head, smile wry. She gestured at the kayak, now fully loaded. "Got everything you need? Enough to eat? Your cell phone juiced up?"

"Yes, dear." He gave a long-suffering sigh. "Quit your worrying. I've done this a time or two."

Rachel's expression softened. She cupped his stubbled jaw, thumb grazing his cheekbone. "I know. Just...be careful out there, okay? Come back to me."

Mark's throat tightened. He covered her hand with his own, squeezing gently. "Always, Rach. Nothing could keep me away from you." The words rang with conviction, a solemn vow.

For a long moment, they simply held each other's gaze, an unspoken conversation passing between them. Then Rachel broke the spell, stretching up on her toes to brush a kiss across his mouth.

"Go on, then." She stepped back, hugging herself. "Go show that river who's boss."

Mark flashed her a crooked grin. "Yes, ma'am." He snapped off a cheeky salute.

As he hauled the kayak out to the car, his phone buzzed insistently in his pocket. He paused, glancing back to make sure Rachel had gone inside. Coast clear, he fished out the device and checked the screen.

The text was short. Cryptic to anyone else, but he understood immediately.

It's time. 1400. Usual spot. Come alone.

Mark stared at the message, jaw clenched. Fuck. It was really happening. After all this, judgement day had finally arrived...

He deleted the text with a vicious jab. Shoving the phone deep in his pocket, he attacked the kayak straps with renewed focus. His movements were sharp, jerky. Agitation simmered under his skin.

But he wouldn't change course now. Couldn't. This ended today, one way or another. Even if it damned his soul to the deepest pits of hell...

Rachel wandered back out, leaning a hip against the garage door frame. She watched him work, head tilted. "You gonna be out there all day again?"

"Why? You miss me already?" Mark shot her a grin over his shoulder, straining to keep his tone light.

"Always." Her smile turned sly. "Mostly I just want to make sure you'll be home in time for dinner. It's taco night, remember?"

"Shit, is it Tuesday already?" He secured the last strap with more force than necessary. "I might be late."

Rachel straightened, brow furrowing. "Late? How come?"

Mark hesitated, mind racing. He hated lying to her, but the truth... Christ, he couldn't lay that burden on her shoulders. Better to carry it alone.

"Just got some errands to run in town afterwards." He busied himself double-checking the kayak, avoiding her searching gaze. "Figured I'd get them out of the way while I'm out."

Silence stretched between them, heavy with unspoken questions. Mark could practically feel Rachel's eyes boring into his back, trying to puzzle him out.

Finally, she sighed. "Fine, keep your secrets. But I expect you to make it up to me later."

The forced levity in her voice made his chest ache. She knew something was off, even if she couldn't put her finger on what. He was hurting her with this evasiveness, and he fucking hated himself for it.

But it was necessary. To keep her safe, keep her out of the crosshairs. He'd walk through fire before he let anyone use her to get to him.

Mark turned to face her, dredging up a shadow of his usual smirk. "Don't I always?"

He crossed to her in two long strides, catching her face between his palms and kissing her fiercely. Rachel made a soft sound of surprise before melting into him, hands fisting in his shirt.

He poured everything he couldn't say into that kiss, branding her with the heat of his desperation. Memorizing the sweet taste of her, the way she fit so perfectly against him.

Like it might be the last time.

With a monumental effort, Mark forced himself to pull away. Rachel blinked up at him, lips parted and eyes dazed. It took every ounce of his willpower not to dive back in, lose himself in her warmth.

But the clock was ticking.

He brushed a thumb over her cheekbone, savoring the silken feel of her skin. "I'll see you tonight, okay? Don't wait up."

Rachel caught his wrist, searching his face. "Be careful out there."

The words carried a weight of meaning, an acknowledgment of the secrets between them. She might not know the details, but she knew him. Knew he was wading into dangerous waters.

Mark swallowed hard, throat suddenly tight. "Always am."

It felt like a lie, bitter on his tongue. But he'd do whatever it took to shield her from the ugliness waiting for him downriver.

Even if it meant shattering her trust in the process.

He pressed a final, fierce kiss to her forehead before pulling away, every step feeling like a mile. The driver's door creaked as he yanked it open, the sound unnaturally loud in the charged silence.

Mark slid behind the wheel, movements mechanically precise. He could feel Rachel's stare burning into his profile as he adjusted the rearview mirror, his own dark eyes glaring back at him in accusation.

Coward. Liar. Selfish bastard.

He deserved every venomous word. But he'd walk through hell a thousand times over if it kept her safe.

The engine grumbled to life, a leashed beast waiting to tear free. He met Rachel's eyes one last time, taking a mental snapshot. Her hesitant smile, the way the morning sun lit her hair in a golden halo.

His personal angel, too good for a sinner like him.

Mark lifted a hand in farewell, the casual gesture belying the storm raging inside him. Rachel mirrored him, her slender fingers fluttering like anxious birds.

Then he was backing down the driveway, tires crunching over gravel. He kept his gaze locked dead ahead, refusing to look in the mirrors. Knowing if he did, his resolve would shatter like spun glass.

The road stretched before him, a black ribbon leading straight into the lion's den. And for the first time in his miserable life, Mark sent up a silent prayer.

Not for himself, but for the woman he was leaving behind. The one bright spot in his dark existence.

"Forgive me, Rachel," he murmured, hands white-knuckled on the steering wheel. "Please, just fucking forgive me."

Then he gunned the engine and roared off down the street, chasing ghosts and demons only he could see.

Palm trees lined the sidewalks, their fronds swaying in the morning breeze like lazy sentinels. Picture-perfect houses stood at attention, each one a cookie-cutter clone of its neighbor. White picket fences, manicured lawns, and pastel paint jobs. The American Dream, packaged and sold in neat little boxes.

Mark's lip curled in a sneer as he navigated the winding streets. This place was a fucking façade, a pretty veneer hiding the rot beneath. He'd learned that lesson the hard way, paid for it with blood and tears.

His gaze flicked to the rearview mirror, half-expecting to see a parade of flashing lights on his tail. But the road behind him was empty, just like the hollow feeling in his chest.

"Get it together, Jennings," he growled, the words harsh in the stillness of the car. "You've got a job to do."

Right. The job. The one that had landed him in this goddamn mess in the first place. Some days, he wondered if it was worth it. If maybe he should just put a bullet in his own head and be done with it.

But then he'd remember the promise he'd made, the one that kept him going when everything else had turned to ash. He'd sworn to protect her, to keep her safe from the monsters that lurked in the shadows.

Even if it meant becoming one himself.

Mark's fingers tightened on the steering wheel as he turned onto the highway, the city skyline rising in the distance like a jagged maw. He let out a slow breath, his mind already racing ahead to the task at hand.

It was going to be a long fucking day.

The highway stretched out before him, a ribbon of asphalt cutting through the sprawling suburbs. Mark gunned the engine, the rumble of the V8 drowning out the thoughts that clawed at the edges of his mind.

He'd always found solace in the open road, the freedom of leaving everything behind. But today, even the promise of escape couldn't ease the tension that coiled in his gut.

His phone buzzed in the cupholder, the screen lighting up with a new message. Mark's jaw clenched as he glanced at the name. Donovan. The man who'd dragged him into this nightmare in the first place.

"Fuck," he muttered, reaching for the phone with a trembling hand.

The message was short, just a set of coordinates and a time. Mark's stomach churned as he read the numbers, his mind already conjuring up images of what he might find at the other end.

He tossed the phone back into the cupholder, his fingers curling around the steering wheel until his knuckles turned white. He'd known what he was getting into when he'd taken the job, but that didn't make it any easier.

The river was waiting for him, a chance to clear his head before the real work began. He'd always found peace on the water, the rhythmic dip and pull of the paddle, the gentle sway of the kayak beneath him.

But even as he pictured the tranquil scene, he couldn't shake the feeling that something was wrong. The coordinates Donovan had sent him were in the middle of nowhere, miles from any town or city.

What the hell was he walking into?

Mark shook his head, trying to push the thought aside. He'd figure it out when he got there. For now, he needed to focus on the task at hand.

The kayak was waiting for him at the river's edge, a silent sentinel guarding the secrets of the water. Mark pulled into the gravel lot, his tires crunching against the loose stones.

He climbed out of the car, the cool morning air filling his lungs as he stretched his legs. The river was a mirror, the surface so still it seemed almost unnatural.

But beneath that calm exterior, Mark knew the currents ran deep. He'd seen firsthand the kind of darkness that could lurk beneath the surface, waiting to pull you under.

He wouldn't let that happen. Not again.

With a grim set to his jaw, Mark began unloading his gear, his movements precise and efficient. He had a job to do, and he'd be damned if he let anything get in his way.

Even if it killed him.

Mark secured the kayak to the top of his car, double-checking the straps to ensure it wouldn't budge during the drive. The highway stretched out before him, a ribbon of asphalt cutting through the lush green landscape. He merged onto the road, the engine humming as he accelerated.

The familiar routine of the journey settled over him like a well-worn coat. The miles ticked by, the scenery blurring into a kaleidoscope of colors. But even as he drove, Mark couldn't shake the nagging sense of unease that had taken root in his gut.

He glanced at his phone, the screen dark and silent. No new messages. No updates from Donovan. Just a set of coordinates and a cryptic warning to come alone.

"What the hell are you playing at, Donovan?" Mark muttered under his breath, his fingers tightening on the steering wheel.

He'd known Donovan for years, ever since their days in the military. The man was a ghost, a shadow who moved in the darkest corners of the world. If he was reaching out, it could only mean one thing.

Trouble.

Mark's mind raced with possibilities, each more unsettling than the last. Was it a trap? A setup? Or something worse?

He shook his head, trying to clear his thoughts. Speculation would get him nowhere. He needed facts, hard evidence. And the only way to get that was to keep driving.

The highway stretched on, an endless ribbon of gray. Mark settled in for the long haul, his eyes fixed on the horizon. Whatever lay ahead, he'd face it head-on.

Just like he always did.

Rachel paced back and forth across the living room, her cell phone gripped tightly in her sweaty palm. She jabbed at the screen, dialing Mark's number for what felt like the hundredth goddamn time. It rang and rang before going to voicemail. Again.

"Fuck!" she hissed under her breath. Her jaw clenched as a potent cocktail of worry and frustration bubbled up inside her. Where the hell was he? This wasn't like Mark at all. He always picked up. Always.

She glanced at the clock. Over four hours since he said he'd be home from his kayaking trip. Four long, agonizing hours of sitting here, waiting, slowly losing her mind. Rachel's stomach churned, her imagination running wild with all the terrible things that could have happened out there on the river.

No. She shook her head forcefully. She couldn't let herself spiral down that path. Not yet. Mark was fine. He had to be. There had to be some logical explanation.

Rachel scrolled through her contacts until she found the number for Mark's favorite kayak rental place upriver. Her finger hovered over the call button as she sucked in a breath, trying to steady herself. Then she tapped it.

"River Riders Kayak Rentals, how can I help you?" a chipper female voice answered after two rings.

"Hi, yes, I'm calling about my husband Mark. Mark Jennings," Rachel said, doing her best to keep her voice calm and level. "He rented a kayak from you guys earlier today for a solo trip and he hasn't come home yet. I'm wondering if you've seen him or heard anything?"

"Let me check with the guys who were working the booth today. Can you hold for just a moment?"

"Of course." Rachel grabbed a pen and notepad from the coffee table, poised to write down anything remotely useful. She gnawed at her bottom lip as tinny hold music played in her ear.

"Ma'am? I checked and the last time anyone remembers seeing your husband was around 11am this morning when he launched his kayak upriver."

Rachel's heart sank like a stone. She scribbled "11am - last seen" on the pad in uneven, frantic strokes. "Okay...and no one saw him return the kayak or his equipment later?"

"No, doesn't look like it. You said he was due back hours ago?"

"Yes," Rachel whispered, the word heavy on her tongue. "Okay. Well, thank you for checking. I appreciate it." She hung up before the woman could reply and tossed the phone on the couch.

Panic rose in her throat like bile. Something was wrong. Something was very, very wrong. Her eyes darted to the window, where outside the last crimson traces of dusk were fading, replaced by the black velvet cloak of nightfall.

Mark was out there somewhere. Alone. And she had no idea where. No idea if he was hurt or lost or...worse. Rachel's heart galloped against her ribcage as grim possibilities swirled in her brain.

She needed help. She couldn't do this by herself anymore. Her gaze fell on her phone laying on the couch cushion. It was time. Time to call for backup. Her hand trembled as she reached for it.

Rachel's fingers hovered over the screen, the three digits blurring through unshed tears. 9-1-1. A call she never thought she'd have to make, not for Mark. Not for her unflappable, adventure-loving husband who knew these rivers like the back of his hand.

But as the minutes ticked by, each one echoing in the oppressive silence of their empty home, Rachel knew she couldn't delay any longer. She had to push past the stubborn part of her that insisted on handling everything alone, the part that recoiled at the thought of admitting she needed help.

With a shaky breath, she tapped out the numbers and pressed the phone to her ear. It rang once, twice, each tone amplifying the dread that coiled in her stomach.

"911, what's your emergency?" The dispatcher's voice was calm, professional, a stark contrast to the chaos swirling inside Rachel's head.

"My husband, he's missing," Rachel said, the words tumbling out in a rush. "He went kayaking this morning and he hasn't come back. It's been hours, and no one's seen him, and I've called everywhere, and—"

THE HUSBAND

"Ma'am, take a deep breath," the dispatcher interrupted gently. "I need you to slow down and give me some more information, okay? What's your husband's name?"

Rachel closed her eyes, forcing herself to inhale slowly. "Mark. Mark Jennings."

"And what time did he leave for his kayaking trip?"

"Around 8:30 this morning. He said he'd be back by 2:00, 3:00 at the latest. But it's past 8:00 now and there's no sign of him." Rachel's voice broke on the last word, tears finally spilling down her cheeks.

"Okay, Mrs. Jennings, I'm sending an officer to your location now. They'll be there shortly to take a full report and start the search. In the meantime, try to stay calm and think if there's any other information you can provide that might help us locate your husband."

Stay calm. The words almost made Rachel laugh. As if calm was an option when the man she loved was lost somewhere in the vast wilderness, his fate unknown. But she swallowed back the hysterical bubble rising in her throat and managed a hoarse "Okay."

"Help is on the way, Mrs. Jennings. We'll do everything we can to find your husband."

The line went dead, and Rachel was alone once more, the weight of her worst fears pressing down on her chest until she could hardly breathe. She looked out the window again, at the inky blackness that had swallowed the street, the trees, the world beyond.

Hold on, Mark, she thought desperately, as if he could hear her silent plea across the miles that separated them. I'm coming. Just hold on.

A sharp rap at the door jolted Rachel from her spiraling thoughts. She hurried to answer it, hope and dread warring in her chest as she turned the knob.

Detective Samantha Reyes stood on the porch, her dark eyes steady and assessing. "Mrs. Jennings? I'm Detective Reyes. May I come in?"

Rachel nodded mutely, stepping aside to allow the detective entry. She took in Reyes' crisp pantsuit, the glint of her badge at her waist, and felt a flicker of relief. This woman exuded competence, a no-nonsense air that suggested she knew exactly what to do.

"Please, sit down," Reyes said, gesturing to the couch. She settled herself in the armchair opposite, pulling out a notepad and pen. "I know this is a difficult time, but I need you to walk me through everything that happened today. Every detail you can remember could be important."

Rachel sank onto the couch, her fingers twisting together in her lap. "Mark left early this morning for a kayaking trip. He said he'd be back by dinner, but he never showed up. I've been calling his phone for hours, but it just goes straight to voicemail."

Reyes nodded, jotting down notes. "Did he mention where exactly he was going? Any specific landmarks or routes?"

"He said he was heading to the river, to the spot where we always launch from. It's about an hour's drive from here." Rachel's voice quavered, and she took a shuddering breath. "I should have gone with him. I should have—"

"Mrs. Jennings." Reyes' voice was gentle but firm. "This is not your fault. We're going to do everything we can to find your husband. Now, can you tell me what he was wearing? What his kayak looks like?"

As Rachel recounted the details, her mind flashed to the last glimpse she'd had of Mark. The sun glinting off his auburn hair, the easy grin he'd flashed her as he loaded his gear into the truck. The memory blurred, and suddenly all she could see was that vast expanse of river, the currents swirling dark and deep.

Oh God, what if he's hurt? What if he's trapped somewhere, or lost, or—

The thoughts clawed at her, razor-sharp talons shredding her composure. A sob tore from her throat, and she pressed a hand to her mouth, trying to hold back the flood. But it was no use. The tears came, hot and fast, a tidal wave of terror and despair that swept her under.

Through the haze of her anguish, she felt Reyes' hand on her shoulder, steady and anchoring. "Breathe, Mrs. Jennings. Just breathe. We're going to find him. I promise you, we will do everything humanly possible to bring your husband home."

Rachel clung to those words like a lifeline, desperate to believe them. Because the alternative was unthinkable, a yawning abyss of loss that threatened to swallow her whole.

Please, she prayed, to any god that might be listening. Please let him be okay. Let him come home to me.

The world beyond the window remained dark and silent, offering no answers. Only the promise of a long night ahead, and the desperate hope that somewhere out there, Mark was fighting his way back to her.

Detective Reyes strode out of the Jennings house, her jaw set with steely determination. She barked orders into her radio, her voice cutting through the night air like a blade.

"I want every available unit down at the riverbank, now. We're launching a full-scale search and rescue operation. Get me helicopters in the air, K-9 units on the ground, and divers in the water. We're not coming back without him."

The response crackled back, a chorus of affirmatives from officers eager to jump into action. Reyes turned to the group of volunteers gathering nearby, their faces etched with worry and resolve.

"Alright, folks, listen up. We've got a missing kayaker out there, and every minute counts. I need you to fan out along the shoreline, eyes peeled for any sign of him or his gear. You see anything, you radio it in immediately. Understood?"

Nods and murmurs of assent rippled through the crowd. Reyes locked eyes with each of them, her gaze unwavering. "Let's bring him home."

As the volunteers dispersed, Reyes pivoted back to her team. "Martinez, coordinate with the dive team. I want those divers in the water ASAP. Johnson, you're on helicopter duty. Keep those birds in the air and those spotlights sweeping. The rest of you, with me. We're going to comb every inch of this goddamn riverbank until we find something."

The officers leapt into motion, a well-oiled machine fueled by adrenaline and purpose. In the distance, the thrum of helicopter blades filled the air, the searchlights piercing the darkness like lances. On the ground, flashlight beams danced across the shoreline, bobbing and weaving as the searchers fanned out.

Reyes paused for a moment, her gaze drawn to the inky black expanse of the river. Somewhere out there, Mark Jennings was waiting to be found. And come hell or high water, she was going to find him.

"Hang on, Mark," she murmured, her words carried away on the breeze. "We're coming for you."

With that, she turned and plunged into the search, her flashlight cutting a determined path through the night. The hunt was on, and failure was not an option. Not on her watch.

Rachel stumbled through the underbrush, her flashlight beam slicing through the darkness like a knife. "Mark!" she called out, her voice raw and desperate. "Mark, where are you?"

The only response was the rustle of leaves and the distant churning of the river. With each step, the sense of helplessness tightened its grip around her heart, squeezing until she could barely breathe.

"Goddammit, Mark," she muttered, blinking back the tears that threatened to blur her vision. "You can't do this to me. You can't just disappear."

The beam of her flashlight caught a glint of something metallic in the dirt. Heart pounding, Rachel scrambled forward, dropping to her knees to grab at the object. It was a keychain, the one she'd given Mark for their anniversary. The sight of it sent a surge of hope through her veins.

"He was here," she whispered, clutching the keychain like a lifeline. "He was fucking here."

A rustling in the bushes behind her made Rachel whirl around, her flashlight beam landing on the face of a young officer. "Ms. Jennings," he said, his voice gentle. "We need you to come back to the command center. Detective Reyes has an update."

Rachel hesitated, her gaze darting back to the river. The urge to keep searching was like a physical ache in her bones. But the officer's words had sparked a flicker of hope in her chest. If Reyes had an update, maybe it meant they'd found something. Maybe it meant they were one step closer to bringing Mark home.

With a nod, Rachel pushed herself to her feet, the keychain still clutched tightly in her fist. "Lead the way," she said, her voice steady despite the tremor in her hands.

As they trudged back through the woods, Rachel's mind raced with possibilities. What if they'd found Mark's kayak? What if they'd discovered a clue that could lead them to him? The not knowing was like a physical weight pressing down on her chest, making it hard to breathe.

At the command center, Reyes was huddled with a group of officers, their faces grim in the harsh glare of the floodlights. Rachel's heart stuttered in her chest as she approached, bracing herself for the worst.

"What is it?" she asked, her voice barely above a whisper. "What did you find?"

Reyes looked up, her expression unreadable. "We found Mark's kayak," she said, her words measured and careful. "It was caught in some branches about a mile downstream."

Rachel's knees buckled, and she grabbed onto the edge of a nearby table for support. "Was he...?" she couldn't finish the question, couldn't give voice to the fear that had been gnawing at her since the moment she'd realized Mark was missing.

Reyes shook her head. "No sign of him yet. But we're not giving up. We've got divers in the water and officers combing the shoreline. We'll find him, Rachel. I promise you that."

Rachel nodded, swallowing hard against the lump in her throat. She believed Reyes. She had to. The alternative was too painful to contemplate.

As the search continued, Rachel stood on the riverbank, her eyes fixed on the dark expanse of water before her. Somewhere out there, Mark was waiting for her. And she would find him. No matter what it took.

Rachel's eyes stung with unshed tears as she turned to face the group of volunteers who had gathered beside her on the riverbank. Their faces were etched with concern, their eyes heavy with the weight of the search that stretched before them. She swallowed hard, forcing a smile that felt like it might crack her face in two.

"Thank you," she said, her voice rough with emotion. "Thank you all for being here. For helping us find Mark. I can't tell you how much it means to me, to all of us."

A woman with silver hair and kind eyes reached out, squeezing Rachel's hand. "We're here for you, honey. We'll do everything we can to bring him home."

Rachel nodded, blinking back the tears that threatened to spill down her cheeks. She looked out over the water, the inky blackness broken only by the beams of flashlights and the flashing red and blue of the police cruisers. Somewhere out there, Mark was waiting for her. She could feel it in her bones.

A sudden commotion caught her attention, and she turned to see Detective Reyes standing at the water's edge, her phone pressed to her ear. Her brow was furrowed, her mouth set in a hard line. Rachel's heart

THE HUSBAND

leapt into her throat as she watched the detective's expression shift from hope to frustration.

"What is it?" Rachel asked, hurrying over to Reyes's side. "Did they find something?"

Reyes shook her head, her jaw clenched tight. "False alarm," she said, her voice clipped. "Some hikers thought they saw something in the water, but it turned out to be a fucking log."

Rachel's shoulders slumped, the brief flicker of hope extinguished as quickly as it had ignited. She ran a hand through her hair, feeling the tangles and snarls that had formed over the long hours of the search.

"Fuck," she muttered, kicking at a rock with the toe of her boot. "Just... fuck."

Reyes placed a hand on Rachel's shoulder, her grip firm and reassuring. "We're not giving up," she said, her eyes blazing with determination. "I don't care if we have to search every inch of this goddamn river. We're going to find him, Rachel. I swear it."

Rachel nodded, drawing strength from the detective's unwavering resolve. She turned back to the water, her gaze sweeping over the murky depths. *Hold on, Mark*, she thought, sending a silent prayer into the night. *I'm coming for you. Just hold on a little longer.*

Rachel slumped down on the riverbank, her legs giving out beneath her as exhaustion and despair took hold. She buried her face in her hands, her breath coming in ragged gasps as the events of the day caught up with her.

Fuck, Mark, where are you? she thought, her mind spinning with the possibilities. *Did you fall in? Did someone hurt you? Are you lying somewhere, broken and bleeding, waiting for me to find you?*

She dug her fingers into the damp soil, the grit embedding itself beneath her nails. The cool earth grounded her, keeping her tethered to reality even as her thoughts threatened to spiral out of control.

Rachel lifted her head, her gaze drawn to the river's inky depths. The water flowed past, indifferent to the drama unfolding on its banks.

Fish swam beneath the surface, their silvery scales catching the moonlight, while insects skated across the top, their delicate wings barely disturbing the surface tension.

Life went on, even in the face of tragedy. Nature didn't give a shit about human suffering, about the agony of not knowing, of imagining the worst.

But Rachel did. She cared so much it felt like her heart was being ripped from her chest with every passing minute.

She closed her eyes, trying to picture Mark's face. His crooked smile, the way his eyes crinkled at the corners when he laughed. The feel of his arms around her, strong and safe and warm.

God, what if she never saw him again? What if this was it, the end of their story?

No. Rachel shook her head, banishing the thought before it could take root. She couldn't think like that. She had to stay strong, to keep believing.

Mark was out there somewhere. And she was going to find him, no matter what it took.

She pushed herself to her feet, wincing as her stiff muscles protested. The search was far from over. The night was just beginning.

Rachel strode back towards the command center, her resolve hardening with every step. She would keep going, keep searching, until she brought Mark home.

Or until she had no choice but to accept the unthinkable.

The darkness deepened as the hours ticked by, the inky black sky seeming to press down on the searchers. Flashlight beams danced across the water's surface, illuminating brief glimpses of floating debris and swirling eddies.

But no sign of Mark.

Rachel felt the tension mounting with every passing minute, the unspoken question hanging heavy in the air. Where was he? What had happened to him?

The possibilities were endless, each more terrifying than the last. And with every hour that slipped away, the chances of a happy ending grew slimmer.

But still, they pressed on. Because giving up was not an option. Not for Rachel, not for Reyes, not for any of the volunteers who had dropped everything to join the search.

They would keep going, keep hoping, until they had an answer.

One way or another.

The siren's wail sliced through the damp morning air as Detective Samantha Reyes slammed the car door and strode toward the riverbank. Controlled chaos greeted her—uniforms swarming the muddy shore, voices crackling over radios, a German shepherd straining against its leash. She clocked the overturned kayak, its hull gashed like a wound. Beside it lay a shattered iPhone, its screen fractured into a spiderweb of cracks.

Reyes intercepted a stocky officer barking orders. "Talk to me, Sarge. What've we got?"

He shook his head. "Not much, Detective. Guy's vanished without a trace. Dogs lost the scent at the water's edge."

"Witnesses? Security cams?"

"Zip. Zero. Nada."

"Fuck." She scanned the churning river, its secrets concealed beneath an impenetrable grey. This didn't track. Something about this whole scene smelled wrong, like three-day-old fish left to rot in the sun.

"Keep your boys on it," she said. "I want every inch of this riverbank searched. Comb the surrounding woods, canvass the area for potential witnesses. Someone must've seen something."

"We're on it," he nodded. "But detective, if he went into that water..."

She held up a hand, cutting him off. "Then we find him. In the meantime, I want that kayak and phone bagged and tagged for forensics."

Her eyes narrowed as she turned back to the water, its surface alive with ripples from the current. The pieces of this puzzle were scattered, taunting her to assemble them. But Samantha Reyes had never met a mystery she couldn't solve. And she sure as hell wasn't about to start now.

Time to dig deeper, shake the trees and see what fell out. Mark Jennings had secrets—that much was clear. And come hell or high water, she'd drag the truth into the unforgiving light of day.

With a last long look at the river, she spun on her heel and headed back to her car. She had work to do.

The door swung open before Reyes could even knock, revealing a red-eyed Rachel Jennings, her face a canvas of grief and confusion. "Detective Reyes? Please, come in. Have you... have you found anything?"

Reyes stepped inside, her keen eyes scanning the living room. Photos of Mark and Rachel adorned the walls, their smiles frozen in happier times. "We're still searching, Mrs. Jennings. I was hoping to ask you a few more questions, if that's alright."

Rachel nodded, leading Reyes to the couch. She perched on the edge, hands clasped tightly in her lap. "Of course. Anything to help find Mark."

Reyes flipped open her notebook, pen poised. "Can you tell me about your relationship with your husband? Any recent changes or issues?"

"No, no issues. We were happy. Mark, he... he adored me." Rachel's voice trembled, tears welling anew. "He'd never just leave like this. Something must have happened to him, I know it."

Reyes jotted down a note, her expression neutral. "And there's nothing else? No arguments, no secrets?"

Rachel's gaze darted away for a split second. "No, nothing like that. We had a perfect life, Detective. Perfect."

The word hung in the air, too polished, too rehearsed. Reyes leaned forward, studying Rachel's face for cracks in the facade. "Mrs. Jennings, I'm here to find the truth. If there's something you're not telling me—"

"I've told you everything," Rachel snapped, her composure slipping. "My husband is missing. Why aren't you out there looking for him instead of interrogating me?"

Reyes held up a placating hand. "I understand your frustration, but I'm just trying to gather all the facts. Even the smallest detail could be important."

Rachel drew a shaky breath, her fingers twisting in her lap. "I'm sorry, I just... I can't believe this is happening. Mark and I, we had plans. A future. And now..."

She dissolved into tears, her shoulders shaking with the force of her sobs. Reyes watched her, pen hovering over the page. Grief, yes. But there was something else lurking beneath the surface. Something that didn't quite fit.

Reyes' instincts prickled, a familiar tug in her gut. Rachel Jennings knew more than she was letting on. The question was, what secrets was she hiding behind those perfect family photos and trembling tears?

Secrets that might just hold the key to unraveling the mystery of Mark Jennings' disappearance. Secrets that Reyes was determined to uncover, one way or another.

She flipped her notebook closed, rising to her feet. "Thank you for your time, Mrs. Jennings. I'll be in touch if we have any further questions."

Rachel nodded, not meeting her eyes. "Please, just... just find him. Bring him home to me."

Reyes inclined her head, a silent promise. Then she was out the door, her mind churning with possibilities. Rachel Jennings and her picture-perfect marriage... what was she hiding?

Time to dig deeper. The truth was out there, waiting to be uncovered. And Samantha Reyes wouldn't rest until she dragged it kicking and screaming into the light.

Detective Reyes fixed Rachel with a probing gaze. "Tell me about Mark's daily routine. His habits, his hobbies. Anything out of the ordinary."

Rachel dabbed at her eyes with a tissue, her voice quavering. "He was always so predictable. Up at 6 AM, out the door by 7:30. He'd grab coffee on the way to the office, put in his hours, then head straight home. Rarely deviated."

"Rarely?" Reyes raised an eyebrow. "So there were exceptions."

"I..." Rachel hesitated, twisting the tissue in her hands. "A few weeks ago, he started coming home later. Said he needed to blow off steam after work."

"Doing what, exactly?"

"Kayaking." The word seemed to catch in Rachel's throat. "He bought a kayak out of the blue, started disappearing for hours at a time. I thought it was just a midlife crisis thing, you know? Something to make him feel alive again."

Reyes leaned forward, her elbows on her knees. "And did it? Make him feel alive again?"

Rachel met her gaze, tears spilling down her cheeks. "I don't know. He seemed... different. Distracted. Like his mind was always somewhere else." She drew a shuddering breath. "I should have seen it. Should have known something was wrong."

Reyes' pen scratched across the page, her thoughts racing. A sudden interest in kayaking, hours unaccounted for... it didn't add up. Not for a man as predictable as Mark Jennings.

She flipped her notebook closed, rising to her feet. "Just one more thing, Mrs. Jennings. I'd like to take a look at Mark's home office, if you don't mind."

Rachel blinked, caught off guard. "His office? Why?"

THE HUSBAND

"Call it a hunch." Reyes gave her a tight smile. "Might help me get a better sense of who your husband was, outside of work and family."

Rachel hesitated, her eyes darting toward the hallway. For a moment, Reyes thought she might refuse. But then she nodded, pushing herself to her feet. "Of course. This way."

She led Reyes down the hallway, past a line of family photos. Smiling faces, frozen in time. A reminder of the life Mark Jennings had left behind.

Rachel paused outside a closed door, her hand on the knob. "I haven't been in here since..." She swallowed hard. "Since he disappeared."

Reyes placed a hand on her shoulder, a gentle reassurance. "I understand. Take your time."

Rachel drew a deep breath, then pushed the door open. The hinges creaked, a sound that seemed to echo in the stillness of the house.

Reyes stepped inside, her eyes sweeping the room. A cluttered desk, stacks of papers, a computer monitor displaying a screensaver of a serene river scene. The pieces of a life interrupted.

She moved to the desk, her fingers skimming over the surface. Searching for something, anything that might shed light on the man Mark Jennings had been.

And then she saw it. A glint of metal, barely visible beneath a stack of papers. A hidden compartment, cleverly concealed in the desk's underside.

Reyes' heart quickened, adrenaline surging through her veins. Her instincts had been right. Mark Jennings had secrets, secrets he'd gone to great lengths to hide.

Secrets that might just hold the key to his disappearance.

She reached for the compartment, her fingers trembling with anticipation. Whatever lay inside, she knew it would change everything.

The truth was waiting. And Samantha Reyes was ready to face it, no matter the cost.

With a quick tug, Reyes pried open the compartment, revealing a sleek, unmarked laptop nestled within. It was an odd find, considering the well-used desktop computer that sat atop the desk.

"What the hell?" Reyes muttered under her breath, her brow furrowing as she lifted the laptop from its hiding place.

Rachel stepped closer, her eyes wide with a mix of curiosity and apprehension. "I've never seen that before. Mark never mentioned having another laptop."

Reyes shot her a sharp glance. "You sure about that? No secret projects, no late-night work sessions?"

Rachel shook her head, her lips pressed into a thin line. "No, nothing like that. He was always open about his work, at least I thought he was..."

The detective turned her attention back to the laptop, running her fingers along the smooth, cool surface. It was top-of-the-line, the kind of machine that screamed money and power.

And secrets. Lots of fucking secrets.

Reyes set the laptop on the desk, her mind racing with possibilities. What was Mark Jennings hiding? And more importantly, why?

She flipped open the screen, her heart pounding in her chest as she hit the power button. The machine whirred to life, the display flickering before

Reyes booted up the unmarked laptop. The screen flickered to life, a luminous glow casting shadows across her intent expression. Her fingers danced over the keys, muscle memory guiding her through bypassing encrypted files and security protocols.

The thrum of the hard drive and the tapping of keys were the only sounds punctuating the tense silence. Reyes' brow furrowed in concentration as she navigated deeper into the laptop's forbidden recesses.

"C'mon you son of a bitch, show me what you're hiding," she muttered under her breath. Anticipation bubbled up inside her, the thrill of uncovering buried secrets setting her nerves alight.

Line after line of code flashed across the screen, a matrix of data rendering into discernible files and images. Reyes' eyes darted back and forth, processing information at breakneck speed.

Then she saw it. Explicit messages filled the screen - a sordid affair spelled out in lurid detail. Correspondence between Mark Jennings and a woman named Irina from Kiev. Reyes' pulse quickened as she took in the damning evidence.

"Gotcha," she whispered, a mix of disbelief and vindication washing over her. She leaned back in the chair, not quite believing what she was seeing. Mark's shiny veneer of devoted husband was starting to crack.

This changed everything. The missing persons case had just morphed into something far more sinister. Reyes knew she had stumbled onto the break she needed, ugly as it was. Her instincts had been dead-on.

She took a swig of now-cold coffee, mind racing through the implications. The laptop was the key to blowing this whole charade wide open. Reyes allowed herself a brief, grim smile. However this played out, the truth was going to come out - and it wasn't going to be pretty.

Reyes sat motionless, eyes locked on the screen, her thoughts a churning maelstrom. The weight of the revelation settled heavily on her shoulders, the implications staggering. Mark Jennings, the seemingly devoted husband, had been living a double life, carrying on a clandestine affair with a woman halfway around the world.

"Fuck," Reyes muttered under her breath, running a hand through her hair. She couldn't shake the nagging feeling that this was just the tip of the iceberg. What other secrets was Mark hiding? How deep did this rabbit hole go?

Her mind raced with questions, each one more unsettling than the last. Was the affair a motive for disappearance? A catalyst for something more sinister? Or was it just a sordid detail in a tapestry of lies?

Reyes' heart ached for Rachel, knowing the devastating impact this revelation would have. The illusion of a perfect marriage, shattered in an instant. The betrayal would cut deep, leaving scars that might never fully heal.

She took a deep breath, steeling herself for the difficult road ahead. This was the part of the job she hated most - watching the fallout of someone else's selfish choices. But she couldn't let empathy cloud her judgment. She had a duty to uncover the truth, no matter how ugly it might be.

Reyes reached for her phone, her fingers hovering over the keypad. She needed to call in a tech team, to secure the laptop as evidence. But for a moment, she hesitated, the weight of responsibility bearing down on her.

"Get it together, Reyes," she muttered, shaking off the momentary doubt. She dialed the number, her voice steady and professional as she relayed the necessary information. But even as she spoke, her mind was already three steps ahead, strategizing the next moves in the investigation.

The game had changed, the stakes higher than ever. Reyes knew she couldn't afford to miss a single detail, to overlook any potential lead. She had to be smarter, faster, more relentless than ever before.

As she ended the call, Reyes leaned back in the chair, her gaze drifting to the family photos lining the walls. The smiling faces seemed to mock her now, a cruel reminder of the facade that had just crumbled.

She stood abruptly, a renewed sense of determination coursing through her veins. She wouldn't rest until she had uncovered the truth, no matter where it led. Mark Jennings had secrets - and Reyes was going to drag them all into the light.

THE HUSBAND

The tech team arrived in a flurry of activity, their faces a mix of curiosity and professionalism. Reyes stepped aside, allowing them to swarm the office, their gloved hands carefully cataloging and bagging each piece of evidence.

She slipped outside, desperate for a moment of fresh air. The porch boards creaked beneath her feet as she leaned against the railing, her gaze sweeping over the quiet suburban street. It was a picture of tranquility, a stark contrast to the chaos swirling inside her mind.

Reyes pulled out a cigarette, her fingers trembling slightly as she lit it. She inhaled deeply, the nicotine rush doing little to calm her racing thoughts. The messages between Mark and Irina played on a loop in her head, each word a damning indictment of a man she had once respected.

But there was more to this story, Reyes could feel it in her bones. The pieces didn't quite fit, the edges too jagged, the picture too incomplete. She needed to dig deeper, to peel back the layers of deception until she reached the rotten core.

Her eyes narrowed as she caught sight of a neighbor peering through their curtains, their face a mask of curiosity and suspicion. Reyes flicked her cigarette, watching as the ash drifted to the ground. Let them talk, let them whisper their rumors and speculation. She had a job to do, and she wouldn't be swayed by idle gossip.

As she turned to head back inside, Reyes squared her shoulders, her resolve hardening with each step. She would unravel this mystery, would follow the trail of lies and deceit until she uncovered the truth. No matter how deep the rabbit hole went, no matter how ugly the reality might be, she would not rest until justice was served.

The game was on, and Reyes was ready to play.

Detective Samantha Reyes squinted bleary eyes at the glowing computer screen. Her desk was a mess of scattered case files, empty coffee cups, and junk food wrappers. The only light came from the damning words illuminated before her - the explicit messages and photos Mark Jennings had exchanged with his Ukrainian mistress, Irina.

"You stupid, selfish bastard," Reyes muttered under her breath, clicking through the sordid evidence of Mark's double life. Each intimate detail twisted the knife of betrayal deeper. This asshole had a loving wife and family at home while he was off playing 007 with his side piece. Now Reyes had to clean up the shitshow he left behind.

She sighed and reached for her cell phone. Her thumb hovered over the contact: Rachel Jennings. Mark's wife. The poor woman had no idea the bomb that was about to drop on her perfect suburban life.

Reyes took a deep breath and hit Call. It rang twice before a cheery female voice answered.

"Hello?"

"Rachel, it's Detective Reyes."

"Oh, hello Detective! Have you found Mark? Is he okay?" Rachel's voice was full of hope and desperation. It made Reyes' chest tighten.

"Rachel, I..." Reyes paused, considering her next words carefully. No gentle way to put this. "We found some things on Mark's computer. Messages and photos...with another woman. I'm so sorry but it looks like Mark was having an online affair with someone in Ukraine."

Silence on the other end. Reyes could picture Rachel's stricken face, her brain struggling to process this horrible revelation about the man she thought she knew. When Rachel finally spoke, her voice quavered with barely contained emotion.

"An affair? I don't - I don't understand. There must be some mistake..."

Reyes sighed. "I wish there was. But the evidence is pretty clear cut."

She glanced back at the explicit sexts glowing accusingly on her screen. The skeevy prick couldn't even be original - "I want to taste every inch of you"? He probably copy-pasted that to a dozen cam girls.

"What evidence?" Rachel demanded. "No, I'm sorry, I just can't believe Mark would ever—"

THE HUSBAND

"Rachel," Reyes cut her off, not unkindly but firmly. "He was sending this woman money. A lot of it. And the messages..." She swallowed hard. "They're very graphic. It was a full-blown online affair. I know this is a hell of a thing to process, but you deserve the truth."

She heard a sharp intake of breath and then muffled sobbing on the other end. Reyes closed her eyes, silently cursing Mark Jennings to the depths of hell for putting her in this position. For putting his wife through this nightmare.

"I'm so sorry, Rachel. I really am." The words felt inadequate, but it was all Reyes could offer.

After a few shuddering breaths, Rachel managed to choke out: "I - I have to go. I can't—"

"I understand," Reyes said gently. "Listen, take some time but call me if you need anything, okay? Anything at all."

"I will. Thank you, Detective."

The line went dead. Reyes slowly lowered the phone, a heavy, sick feeling settling in her gut. Delivering devastating news was always the hardest part of the job. But this particular betrayal cut deep, even for a hardened cop like her.

She looked back at the messages, disgust twisting her mouth. Reading the intimate exchanges felt like peeping in a sleazy window, but Reyes forced herself to study them clinically. To set aside her revulsion and anger and focus on the facts.

Because under all the pornographic poetry and emojis, something didn't add up. The timing of the affair, the large sums of money, Mark's sudden disappearance ...Reyes' well-honed detective instincts nagged at her. The pieces of the puzzle were scattered in front of her, if she could just arrange them the right way.

She cracked her knuckles and opened up a new spreadsheet. Time to follow the money trail. Mark Jennings wasn't going to slither out of this mess so easily, not if Detective Reyes had anything to say about it. She'd get to the bottom of this sordid mystery. For Rachel's sake, if nothing else.

With a cold, determined focus, Reyes started charting the dates and dollar amounts of Mark's wire transfers to the Ukraine, chasing the digital breadcrumbs he'd carelessly left behind. This creep's reckoning was long overdue. And Detective Samantha Reyes would be the one to deliver it.

Rachel's world spun as Detective Reyes' words sank in like poison darts. Mark, her Mark, entangled with some Ukrainian woman half his age? Sexting like a hormonal teenager when he was supposed to be on a business trip? It defied belief.

"Are you...are you sure?" Her voice came out small and brittle. "Maybe it's some mistake, maybe his phone was hacked or..."

Reyes' sigh crackled over the line. "I'm sorry, Rachel. I really am. But the evidence is pretty damn clear. It's been going on for months."

Months. Rachel sank onto the bed, photos of her and Mark smiling from the dresser. Memories of their life together flickered through her mind like old film reels. Their wedding day, the births of Josh and Lily, anniversaries and holidays and a thousand little everyday moments.

Had it all been a lie? The man in those pictures, the one who'd held her, made love to her, promised forever...she couldn't reconcile him with this new image of a cheating scumbag Reyes painted.

"What about the kids?" Rachel asked hollowly. "What am I supposed to tell them?"

"One thing at a time," Reyes said. "Let's focus on finding Mark first, okay? I promise I'm going to get to the bottom of this. You just...take care of yourself. I'll be in touch soon."

The detective hung up, leaving Rachel marooned in a sea of shock and betrayal. She stared at their wedding photo until her vision blurred and a wail built in her chest. How could he do this? To her, to their family?

The tears came hard and fast then, fifteen years worth. She curled up on Mark's side of the bed and wept, inhaling the scent of his cologne on the pillow. Clinging to the tattered remains of the life she'd thought they'd built. Wondering if she'd ever known the man she married at all.

Detective Reyes stared at the phone in her hand for a long moment after ending the call with Rachel Jennings. Christ, that had been rough. Delivering bad news was part of the job, but devastating a wife and mother, shattering a family with a few blunt sentences...it never got easier.

But dwelling on it was a luxury she couldn't afford right now. Reyes had work to do, a shady husband to track down. She cracked her knuckles and opened up a new spreadsheet on her computer. Time to follow the money.

She entered the dates and dollar amounts of each wire transfer from Mark Jennings' bank account to Irina Volkov in Ukraine. Five thousand here, ten thousand there, all under the guise of "business expenses." Did he really think no one would notice him funneling money to his side piece?

Reyes snorted derisively. For such a successful businessman, Mark had been pretty sloppy covering his tracks. But then, arrogance and stupidity often went hand in hand with pricks like him.

The transfers went back nearly eight months. Mapping them out, a pattern began to emerge. They'd started out small and infrequent, a couple grand now and then. But in the past few weeks, the amounts had increased dramatically, with Mark moving over fifty thousand dollars right before his disappearance.

Reyes frowned at the screen. That was the part that didn't sit right. If this was just a run-of-the-mill affair, albeit a pricey one, why the sudden cash dump and vanishing act? What was Mark up to?

She copied the figures into her report, noting the banks, account numbers, anything that might help track where the money had gone.

When she found this weasel - and she would find him - Reyes would have some pointed questions about his extracurricular activities.

Her phone buzzed with an incoming email - the cyber crimes guy, with his analysis on Mark's digital footprint. Maybe he'd found something to shed light on this shadowy mistress and Mark's endgame.

Reyes smiled grimly. Buckle up, Mr. Jennings. The hunt was on now. And Detective Samantha Reyes never let her prey slip away.

A sharp rap on her door snapped Reyes out of her thoughts. She looked up to see Jack Dennison, the cyber crimes expert, looming in the doorway. His silver hair and weathered face told of countless hours spent staring at screens, unraveling digital deceptions.

"Detective Reyes," he said, his voice gruff. "Got your email. Thought I'd come down personally."

Reyes waved him in. "Appreciate it, Jack. This case is a real clusterfuck."

Dennison settled into the chair opposite her desk, eyeing the files strewn across it. "Aren't they all? What've you got?"

Reyes slid a folder toward him. "Mark Jennings. Disappeared two days ago. Wife thought he was on a business trip, but turns out he's been funneling money to some Ukrainian bombshell."

Dennison flipped through the papers, his brow furrowing. "Sizable transfers. Any idea what for?"

"Not yet. But here's where it gets interesting." Reyes tapped her screen. "Mark's been careful, but not careful enough. I've traced the payments to an account in Kyiv. And the day before he vanished? He moved fifty grand."

Dennison let out a low whistle. "That's no pocket change. You thinking he's pulled the ripcord? Staged his own disappearance to start a new life with his side piece?"

Reyes leaned back, chewing her lip. "It's a theory. But I need more to go on. That's where you come in."

THE HUSBAND 33

She fixed Dennison with a pointed stare. "I need you to dig deeper. Comb through every byte of Mark's digital life. If there's even a hint of evidence that he faked his death, I want to know."

Dennison nodded, his fingers already twitching with the urge to unravel the puzzle. "I'm on it. Give me a day or two to work my magic."

He rose, taking the folder with him. Pausing at the door, he glanced back. "If this guy did orchestrate his own vanishing act, he's in for a world of hurt when you catch up to him."

A fierce smile tugged at Reyes' lips. "Oh, I'm counting on it."

As Dennison's footsteps faded down the hall, Reyes turned back to her screen. The Ukrainian account number glowed mockingly.

"Where are you, Mark?" she muttered. "What game are you playing?"

Her mind raced with possibilities, each more troubling than the last. Was this a simple case of a man running off with his mistress? Or was there something more sinister at play?

Reyes' gut told her there was more to this story. And her instincts were rarely wrong.

She cracked her knuckles, determination surging through her veins. Whatever twisted web Mark Jennings had woven, she would unravel it. Thread by thread, until the truth lay bare.

And then, there would be a reckoning.

Rachel sat motionless on the living room couch, a framed photo clutched tight to her chest. Tears streamed down her face, carving mascara-stained rivers across her cheeks. The smiling faces in the picture blurred, distorted by the sheen of moisture in her eyes.

Mark. Her husband. The father of their children. The man she'd pledged her life to.

A liar. A cheat. A fucking ghost.

Rachel's fingers dug into the frame, the sharp edges biting into her palms. The pain was a welcome distraction from the agony shredding her heart.

How could he do this? How could he betray their family, their love, their future? For what? Some Ukrainian whore he'd met online?

A strangled sob tore from her throat. She wanted to scream, to rage, to break every damn memory of him in this house.

But she couldn't move. Couldn't breathe. Couldn't think beyond the suffocating weight of his betrayal.

The shrill ring of her phone shattered the silence. Rachel flinched, the photo tumbling from her grasp. She stared at the caller ID, her vision blurred by fresh tears.

Detective Reyes.

With a shaking hand, Rachel brought the phone to her ear.

"Rachel, it's Samantha Reyes. I have some new information about Mark's case."

Rachel swallowed hard, her voice a broken whisper. "What is it?"

"We have reason to believe that Mark's disappearance was not an accident. The evidence suggests he may have staged his own death."

The words hit Rachel like a physical blow. She doubled over, bile rising in her throat.

"W-What? Why would he...I don't understand."

"We're still piecing it together," Reyes said, her tone gentle but firm. "But the digital trail indicates he's been transferring large sums of money to an account in Ukraine. The same country where Irina, the woman he was messaging, lives."

Ukraine. Irina. The pieces clicked into place, each one a dagger to Rachel's already bleeding heart.

"So what now?" she choked out, her free hand balling into a fist. "What do we do?"

"I've issued an international alert for Mark," Reyes replied, the steel returning to her voice. "I'm working with authorities here and abroad to track his movements. If he's out there, we'll find him."

Rachel nodded, even though Reyes couldn't see her. "Find him," she whispered, her words laced with equal parts anguish and fury. "Find him and bring him back. I need to look him in the eye and ask him why. Why he destroyed our family. Why he threw away everything we had."

"I will, Rachel. I promise you that."

The line went dead, but Rachel barely noticed. She sat there, amidst the shattered remnants of her life, and let the rage consume her.

Mark had made his choice. And now, he would face the consequences.

No matter how far he ran, no matter how deep he hid, she would make sure he paid for what he'd done.

Even if it meant tearing the world apart to find him.

The harsh fluorescent lights cast an eerie glow over the conference room as Detective Reyes stood before her assembled team. The air was thick with tension, the weight of the case bearing down on every person in the room.

"Listen up," Reyes barked, her voice cutting through the silence like a knife. "We've got a new lead on the Jennings case. Our cyber-crimes expert just uncovered evidence that suggests Mark Jennings may have faked his own death."

A murmur rippled through the room, a mix of surprise and skepticism. Reyes held up a hand, silencing them.

"I know it sounds far-fetched, but the facts don't lie. We've got financial transfers to an account in Ukraine, the same country where Mark was carrying on an online affair. And now, our expert has found inconsistencies in the data that point to a carefully orchestrated disappearance."

She paused, letting the information sink in. "So here's what we're going to do. Johnson, I want you to coordinate with international authorities. Liaise with law enforcement in Ukraine and see if they can track down this Irina woman. If she's involved, I want to know about it."

Johnson nodded, his jaw set with determination. "On it, boss."

"Thompson, you're on forensics. I want every shred of evidence from Mark's office and home analyzed. If there's anything that can tell us where he might have gone, I want it found."

Thompson gave a curt nod, already mentally cataloging the evidence.

The cyber-crimes expert's fingers flew over the keyboard, his eyes locked on the multiple screens flickering with data. Lines of code scrolled by, interspersed with images and timestamps.

"C'mon, you bastard. Show me what you're hiding," he muttered under his breath. With each passing minute, the puzzle pieces fell into place. Money trails led through labyrinthine offshore accounts. IP addresses bounced across continents. A web of deception unraveled before his eyes.

He leaned back, a triumphant smirk on his weathered face. "Gotcha, asshole. Faked your own death and ran off with the mistress, huh? Not on my watch."

He reached for his phone, dialing Detective Reyes. "Hey, Samantha. That hunch of yours? Dead on. This prick staged the whole thing. I've got enough evidence here to nail his coffin shut, even if the son of a bitch ain't really dead."

Reyes sighed heavily, rubbing her bleary eyes. She glanced at the clock - 2:47 AM. The glow of the computer screen illuminated the scattered files on her desk, a chaotic mosaic of Mark Jennings' betrayal.

She'd been poring over the evidence for hours, trying to make sense of it all. The secret messages, the hidden bank accounts, the carefully orchestrated digital trail. It was a tangled web, but with each passing minute, the strands were beginning to unravel.

"Thanks, Mick. Send everything you've got. I want this airtight." She hung up, a renewed sense of determination surging through her veins.

Reyes stood, stretching her aching muscles. She walked to the precinct's coffee maker, pouring a fresh cup of the sludge they called

THE HUSBAND

caffeine. As the bitter liquid scalded her throat, she stared at the corkboard on the wall, Mark Jennings' face staring back at her from a dozen different angles.

She approached the board, pinning up the latest findings. The money transfers, the burner phones, the fake passport. Piece by piece, the puzzle came together, painting a picture of a man desperate to escape his own life.

"Where are you, Mark?" she whispered, her eyes narrowing. "What was so goddamn terrible that you had to leave it all behind?"

She stepped back, her gaze sweeping over the evidence one last time. Tomorrow, she'd brief the team, set the wheels in motion to track Jennings down. But tonight, in the stillness of the empty precinct, Samantha Reyes allowed herself a moment to feel the weight of it all - the lies, the betrayal, the shattered lives left in Mark Jennings' wake.

She drained her coffee cup, crushing it in her fist. "I'm coming for you, you sonofabitch. You can't run forever."

Reyes stood by the precinct window, the city lights twinkling in the distance. She pressed her forehead against the cool glass, exhaustion seeping into her bones. The case had consumed her, every waking moment dedicated to unraveling the twisted web Mark Jennings had woven.

She thought of Rachel, the pain in her voice still echoing in Reyes' mind. The betrayal, the heartbreak - it was a familiar story, one Reyes had seen play out too many times. But this time, it was personal. She'd made a promise to Rachel, a vow to find the truth, no matter how ugly it might be.

"Goddamn you, Mark," Reyes muttered, her breath fogging the glass. "You couldn't just be a run-of-the-mill cheating bastard, could you? Had to go and fake your own fucking death."

She turned away from the window, her gaze falling on the corkboard once more. The evidence was damning, the cyber-crimes expert confirming what Reyes had suspected all along. Mark Jennings was alive, and he was on the run.

Reyes' phone buzzed, jarring her from her thoughts. She glanced at the screen, her heart skipping a beat as she read the message.

"Possible sighting of suspect at Istanbul airport. Passport flagged under alias 'Michael Jensen.'"

Reyes' pulse quickened, adrenaline coursing through her veins. This was it, the break she'd been waiting for. She grabbed her jacket, her fingers already dialing her captain's number.

"Cap, it's Reyes. We've got a lead on Jennings. He's in Istanbul." She paused, listening to the gruff voice on the other end. "I'm on my way to the airport now. I'll keep you posted."

She ended the call, her mind racing. Istanbul. It made sense. A city straddling two continents, a melting pot of cultures and hidden agendas. The perfect place for a man like Mark Jennings to disappear.

Reyes strode out of the precinct, the cool night air hitting her face. She climbed into her car, gunning the engine. As she sped through the empty streets, she felt a flicker of something she hadn't felt in a long time - hope.

"I'm coming for you, Mark," she whispered, her eyes fixed on the road ahead. "You can't hide forever. Not from me."

And with that, Detective Samantha Reyes set off into the night, ready to follow the trail wherever it might lead. The hunt was on, and she wouldn't rest until Mark Jennings was brought to justice.

The hot Texas sun beat down on the busy intersection of Sixth and Congress. Sweat poured from Mark Jennings' brow as he stumbled aimlessly along the sidewalk, nearly colliding with a well-dressed businessman who shot him a disgusted look.

"Watch where you're going, pal," the man sneered, sidestepping Mark's tattered form.

Mark blinked, disoriented. Where the hell am I? He glanced around wildly, taking in the unfamiliar storefronts and gawking faces of passersby. His head throbbed and his mouth felt like it was stuffed with cotton.

Across the street, a young woman in a sundress pointed at Mark, then pulled out her phone. "Yeah, I think it's him. Looks just like that missing person photo they showed on the news."

Within minutes, the wail of police sirens pierced the muggy air. Two patrol cars screeched to a halt at the curb. Four officers emerged, hands hovering near the holsters at their hips as they approached Mark.

"Sir, I need you to put your hands up where we can see them," barked the lead cop, a beefy guy with a blond buzz cut.

"What? Why?" Mark raised his hands, his heart hammering against his ribs. "What's going on?"

The other officers fanned out, forming a loose semi-circle. Their eyes flicked from Mark to the gathering crowd of onlookers.

Buzz Cut took a step closer. "Are you Mark Jennings?"

"Yeah, but—"

"Turn around and place your hands behind your back."

Cold metal cuffs snapped around Mark's wrists. He strained his neck, trying to catch a glimpse of the cop's face.

"Hey, what the hell, man? I didn't do anything wrong! I was just walking—"

The officers hustled him towards the waiting squad car. Mark stumbled, his head still spinning. *This has to be some kind of sick joke. A case of mistaken identity. Any second now they'll realize they've got the wrong guy.*

But as the car door slammed shut behind him, a sinking feeling settled in Mark's gut. He was in deep shit. And he had no idea why.

Miles away in Seattle, Detective Samantha Reyes leaned back in her chair, the bullpen's fluorescent lights casting harsh shadows across the scattered case files on her desk. She reached for her coffee mug, grimacing as the lukewarm sludge hit her tongue.

The shrill ring of her cell phone shattered the relative quiet. Reyes snatched it up, frowning at the unfamiliar number. "Detective Reyes."

"Detective, this is Officer Chad Thompson with the Austin PD. We have a man in custody who we believe to be Mark Jennings."

Reyes bolted upright, her mug clattering onto the desk. "What? Are you sure it's him?"

"Matches the description and ID, ma'am. We're holding him for questioning now."

A surge of adrenaline chased away the lingering fog of exhaustion. Reyes' mind kicked into overdrive. Mark Jennings. In Austin. 1,500 fucking miles from where he'd supposedly died.

She glanced at the wall clock. Nearly midnight. "I'll be on the next flight out. Don't let him out of your sight."

Reyes ended the call and sprang into action, shoving files into her bag and reaching for her jacket. Her mind raced as she headed for the parking lot, the pieces of the puzzle shifting and rearranging themselves.

If Jennings was alive, then what really happened on that kayaking trip? And why the hell would he run to Texas of all places?

Gravel crunched beneath her boots as Reyes climbed into her truck. She cranked the engine, the familiar rumble steadying her nerves. First things first—she needed to get her ass to Austin. Then she'd drag the truth out of Jennings, one way or another.

As she peeled out of the lot, Reyes couldn't shake the feeling that this case was about to blow wide open. And she'd be damned if she wasn't there to see it through.

The Austin Police Department buzzed with activity as Reyes strode through the front doors, her leather jacket flapping behind her. She flashed her badge at the front desk. "Detective Reyes. I'm here for the Jennings interrogation."

The officer on duty looked up, his eyes widening slightly. "Right this way, ma'am."

THE HUSBAND 41

Reyes followed him down the hallway, the fluorescent lights casting harsh shadows across the scuffed linoleum. She could feel the stares and whispers of the local cops as she passed. Her reputation had a habit of preceding her.

The officer stopped outside the interrogation room. "He's all yours, Detective."

Reyes nodded, her hand already on the doorknob. She stepped inside, the heavy door swinging shut behind her with a thud.

Mark Jennings sat hunched at the metal table, his wrists cuffed in front of him. His clothes were rumpled and dirty, his hair a disheveled mess. He looked up as Reyes entered, his bloodshot eyes meeting hers.

Reyes pulled out the chair across from him and sat down, her movements deliberate and precise. She studied Jennings' face, taking in the dark circles under his eyes and the days-old stubble on his jaw. He looked like hell.

She leaned back, crossing her arms over her chest. "Mark Jennings. You've caused quite a stir."

Jennings licked his chapped lips. "I don't... I don't understand what's happening."

Reyes raised an eyebrow. "That makes two of us." She leaned forward, her elbows on the table. "Let's start with the obvious. Why aren't you dead?"

Jennings blinked, confusion etched across his features. "Dead? Why would I be dead?"

"Oh, I don't know. Maybe because you allegedly drowned in a kayaking accident three months ago." Reyes' voice dripped with sarcasm. "Ring any bells?"

Jennings shook his head, his cuffed hands trembling. "No, that's not... I don't remember any of that."

Reyes studied him, her gut telling her there was more to this story. Jennings' bewilderment seemed genuine, but she'd been fooled before. She needed to dig deeper, peel back the layers until she got to the truth.

She reached into her jacket pocket and pulled out a small recorder, placing it on the table between them. "Let's start from the beginning. And don't leave anything out."

Reyes hit the record button, the soft click echoing in the stark room. She fixed Jennings with a penetrating stare, ready to unravel the mystery that had brought her halfway across the country.

One way or another, she'd get to the bottom of this. And God help Mark Jennings if he tried to stand in her way.

Reyes leaned back in her chair, her eyes never leaving Jennings. "So, tell me about this alleged affair."

Jennings' brow furrowed. "Affair? I'm not having an affair. I love my wife."

"Funny, that's not what the evidence suggests." Reyes pulled out a stack of photos from a manila folder, spreading them across the table. "Care to explain these?"

Jennings looked down at the grainy images, his face a mask of confusion. The photos showed him, or someone who looked eerily similar, in compromising positions with a woman who definitely wasn't his wife. "I don't... Those aren't me. I swear, I've never seen that woman before in my life."

Reyes' frustration mounted. She'd seen plenty of cheating spouses try to lie their way out of a tight spot, but something about Jennings' denial felt different. His confusion seemed to run deeper than just a guilty conscience.

She decided to switch gears. "Okay, let's talk about the kayaking trip. What do you remember about that day?"

Jennings closed his eyes, his forehead creasing with the effort to recall. "I remember... I remember getting ready to go out on the water. I had all my gear, my life jacket. But after that, it's just... blank. Like someone wiped my memory clean."

Reyes watched him closely, looking for any signs of deception. But Jennings' body language, his tone, everything about him screamed

THE HUSBAND

sincerity. She couldn't shake the feeling that she was missing something crucial, a piece of the puzzle that would make everything fall into place.

She glanced down at the photos, then back up at Jennings. "If you're not the man in these pictures, then who is he? And how did he end up with your face, your clothes, your whole damn life?"

Jennings met her gaze, his eyes wide and haunted. "I don't know. But I need to find out. Because if that's not me, then who the hell am I?"

Reyes felt a chill run down her spine. She'd worked plenty of cases, seen her fair share of twists and turns. But this? This was something else entirely. And she had a sinking feeling that they were just scratching the surface of a mystery that ran far deeper than either of them could imagine.

Mark's hands clenched into fists, his knuckles whitening as he fought to control his rising anger. "I'm telling you the truth, damn it! I don't know anything about a kayaking incident or an affair. This is all some kind of sick joke or a case of mistaken identity. You have to believe me!"

Reyes leaned back in her chair, her eyes narrowing as she studied Mark's face. She'd seen plenty of desperate men in her time, heard every plea of innocence under the sun. But there was something different about Mark, a raw honesty that unsettled her.

She tapped her finger on the table, her mind racing. *Could he be telling the truth? Or is this just another elaborate lie, a last-ditch attempt to wriggle out of the consequences of his actions?*

Mark's voice broke through her thoughts, his tone now edged with a pleading desperation. "Detective Reyes, please. I'm begging you. Look into my eyes and tell me if you think I'm lying. I swear on everything I hold dear, I have no idea what's going on here."

Reyes met his gaze, searching for any flicker of deceit. But all she saw was a man at his wit's end, a man whose world had been turned upside down. She sighed heavily, her resolve wavering.

Damn it, Reyes. You're getting soft. This guy's good, but they all are. You can't let him get in your head.

She straightened up, her voice firm as she pushed aside her doubts. "Mark Jennings, based on the evidence we have, I have no choice but to place you under arrest for the disappearance of your wife and the alleged affair. You have the right to remain silent. Anything you say can and will be used against you in a court of law."

Mark's face crumpled, his eyes wide with disbelief. "No, no, no. This can't be happening. I'm innocent, I swear it! You're making a mistake!"

As Reyes reached for her handcuffs, a nagging doubt tugged at the back of her mind. *What if he's telling the truth? What if there's more to this than meets the eye?*

She shook her head, pushing the thought aside. *You can't afford to second-guess yourself, Reyes. Stick to the facts, follow the evidence. Let the chips fall where they may.*

But even as she snapped the cuffs around Mark's wrists, a part of her couldn't help but wonder if she was making the biggest mistake of her career.

The metallic click of the handcuffs echoed through the interrogation room as the officers hauled Mark to his feet. "This is bullshit! I didn't do anything!" he shouted, his voice raw with desperation. "You've got the wrong guy!"

Reyes watched as they dragged him out, his protests reverberating down the hallway. She stood there, frozen, her mind a whirlwind of conflicting thoughts. *Did I just send an innocent man to prison? Or is he playing me like a fiddle?*

She rubbed her temples, the beginnings of a headache throbbing behind her eyes. *Get it together, Reyes. You've got a job to do.*

Hours later, Reyes found herself hunched over her desk, the case files spread out before her like a jigsaw puzzle with missing pieces. She'd

THE HUSBAND

been at it for hours, poring over every scrap of evidence, every witness statement, every damn breadcrumb that might lead her to the truth.

But the more she dug, the more the pieces refused to fit. Mark's alibi checked out. The alleged mistress swore up and down that they'd never even met. And the kayaking incident? A freak accident, by all accounts.

So why does it feel like I'm missing something?

Reyes leaned back in her chair, her eyes burning from the harsh fluorescent lights. She glanced at the clock - 2:37 AM. *Fuck. When did it get so late?*

She reached for her coffee mug, grimacing at the cold, bitter dregs. *Story of my life. Always chasing after the truth, even when it's staring me right in the face.*

Reyes stood up, stretching her aching muscles. She knew she should go home, get some rest. But the thought of facing her empty apartment, the silence broken only by the hum of the fridge, made her skin crawl.

No. I'm not giving up. Not until I get to the bottom of this.

She sat back down, her jaw set with determination. *Alright, Jennings. You want to play games? Let's dance.*

Reyes dove back into the files, her mind racing with possibilities. There had to be something she was missing, some clue that would unravel this whole damn mystery.

And she wouldn't rest until she found it.

The shrill ring of her phone shattered the silence, nearly sending Reyes tumbling out of her chair. She grabbed the receiver, her heart pounding in her chest.

"Reyes."

The voice on the other end was breathless, urgent. "Detective, it's Officer Mendez from Phoenix PD. We've got a situation here."

Reyes frowned, her grip tightening on the phone. "What kind of situation?"

"It's Mark Jennings. We've got a sighting of him, right here in Phoenix."

"What the fuck are you talking about?" Reyes snapped, her exhaustion giving way to irritation. "Mark Jennings is in custody. I just interrogated the bastard myself."

"I know it sounds crazy, but I'm telling you, it's him. We've got multiple witnesses, security camera footage, the works. He's here, Detective. In the flesh."

Reyes felt the room spin around her, her mind reeling with the implications. *How the hell is this possible? Did Jennings have a twin? A doppelganger?*

She shook her head, forcing herself to focus. "Alright, Mendez. I'm on my way. Don't let him out of your sight, you hear me?"

"Yes, ma'am. We've got eyes on him now. He's not going anywhere."

Reyes slammed the phone down, her heart racing with a mix of anticipation and dread. She grabbed her jacket, her keys, her gun.

Here we go again. Just when I thought this case couldn't get any weirder.

She paused at the door, her hand hovering over the light switch. The weight of the mystery pressed down on her, threatening to crush her beneath its impossible weight.

No. I won't let it beat me. I'll get to the bottom of this, even if it kills me.

Reyes flicked off the light, plunging the room into darkness. She strode out into the night, her determination renewed, even as the case grew more bizarre with every passing moment.

Alright, Jennings. You want to play games? Let's see how you like it when I change the rules.

"Jesus Christ," Detective Samantha Reyes muttered under her breath as she paced the cramped interrogation room like a caged animal. The fluorescent lights buzzed and flickered overhead, casting

THE HUSBAND

harsh shadows across the mess of papers strewn over the rickety metal table. None of it made a damn bit of sense.

Reyes snatched up the grainy surveillance photo and held it inches from her face, squinting at the blurry image. Mark Jennings, cocky bastard grin plastered across his mug, exiting a Phoenix gas station three days ago. 732 miles away from the Austin jail cell he was currently rotting in.

"What the f**k?" she hissed, slamming the photo back down. Her temples throbbed as she raked her fingers through her hair. People didn't just magically teleport across state lines. But the evidence glaring up at her told a different story. One that spat in the face of logic and reason.

With a scowl, Reyes gathered up the scattered files and shoved them into a manila folder. Answers. She needed goddamn answers.

The door to the tiny interview room creaked open and a young officer poked his head in. "Detective? The witnesses from Phoenix are ready for you."

Reyes took a deep breath and rolled her neck, vertebrae popping. Time to figure out what the hell was going on.

The Phoenix witnesses shifted nervously in their seats as Reyes settled across from them, the folder slapping against the table. She fixed them with a hard stare. The couple, a skinny college kid with a patchy goatee and his platinum blonde girlfriend, glanced at each other uneasily.

"So," Reyes began, her voice calm but laced with steel, "Walk me through it again. When and where did you see Mark Jennings?"

"It...it was three days ago. At the QuikTrip off McDowell Road," the girl said, worrying her lip between her teeth. "It was definitely him. I remember his eyes."

"That f**ker owes me fifty bucks!" Her boyfriend added, nostrils flaring. "He came into the shop, bought a case of beer and some smokes, then took off without paying me back. I went to school with him. It was Mark, I swear on my life."

Reyes massaged her brow, biting back a sigh. Their certainty clashed against the utter absurdity of it all. "You're absolutely sure? There's no chance it could've been someone else who looked like him?"

"No way, no f**king way," the guy insisted, his leg bouncing under the table. "I've known Mark since we were kids. It was him. I'd bet my left nut on it."

Reyes leaned back in her chair, hands clasped on the table. Their unwavering insistence gave her pause. They were either crazy, lying, or telling the truth. And she sure as hell didn't know which option disturbed her more.

Back in the Austin police station, Mark Jennings slouched in a hard plastic chair, his head bowed and face hidden in his hands. His once crisp shirt was wrinkled and stained, his hair disheveled from running anxious fingers through it. He looked like a man on the brink, exhausted and bewildered by the impossible situation he found himself in.

Reyes entered the room, the door closing with a heavy thud behind her. Mark's head snapped up, his bloodshot eyes meeting hers with a mixture of hope and despair. "Detective, please, you have to believe me," he pleaded, his voice hoarse and tinged with desperation. "I didn't do this. I couldn't have. I was here, in Austin, the whole time. This is insane!"

She held up a hand, silencing him. "Mr. Jennings, I'm trying to make sense of this, but you've got to understand how this looks." She pulled out a chair and sat across from him, the metal screeching against the concrete floor. "We've got multiple witnesses placing you in Phoenix, and now this." She tossed a folder onto the table between them.

THE HUSBAND 49

Mark reached for it, his hands shaking as he flipped it open. His face drained of color as he stared at the grainy black and white photos inside. "What...what the hell is this?"

"CCTV footage from an ATM in Kiev," Reyes said, watching him closely. "Timestamped two days ago. And unless you've got an identical twin you never mentioned, that's you, clear as day, withdrawing cash on the other side of the world."

He shook his head vehemently, his voice rising in pitch. "No, no, that's not possible. I've never even been to Ukraine! This is a mistake, it has to be!"

Reyes leaned forward, elbows on the table. "Then you tell me, Mark. How the f**k do you explain this? Because from where I'm sitting, it looks like you're in a world of shit."

Mark's mouth opened and closed, his eyes wild and desperate as they darted from the damning photos to Reyes' unyielding gaze. "I...I can't. I don't know. But it wasn't me, I swear to God. You have to believe me, please!"

Reyes sat back, her jaw clenched tight. She wanted to believe him, wanted to trust the raw, unfiltered terror in his eyes. But the evidence was piling up, each piece more impossible than the last. And as much as her gut told her something wasn't right, she couldn't ignore the facts staring her in the face.

She stood abruptly, the chair scraping loudly across the floor. "I'll be back. Don't go anywhere." The words tasted bitter on her tongue, a harsh reminder of the absurdity of it all.

As she stepped out of the room, the door slamming shut behind her, Reyes leaned against the wall and closed her eyes. Her mind raced, trying to make sense of the senseless. Mark Jennings, in three places at once. Witnesses swearing on their lives. Grainy footage from halfway around the world. None of it made sense, and yet there it was, mocking her with its impossibility.

She took a deep breath, steeling herself. Whatever the hell was going on, she was going to get to the bottom of it. Even if it meant questioning everything she thought she knew about the world and her place in it.

Rachel Jennings stared at the screen, her hands trembling as she gripped the edges of the desk. The grainy CCTV footage played on a loop, each repetition driving the impossible truth deeper into her mind. There he was, her husband, Mark, withdrawing cash from an ATM in Kiev. Thousands of miles away from where he was supposedly being held in custody.

"That's him," she whispered, her voice cracking with emotion. "That's Mark. I know it's him. I'd know him anywhere."

Detective Reyes stood behind her, arms crossed, her brow furrowed as she studied the footage. She'd seen a lot of strange things in her years on the force, but this... this was something else entirely.

"Mrs. Jennings, I understand this is difficult, but we need to consider the possibility that—"

"It's not a possibility," Rachel snapped, her eyes never leaving the screen. "It's the truth. That man, right there, is my husband. I don't care what your evidence says. I know what I'm seeing."

Reyes sighed, running a hand through her hair. She wanted to believe Rachel, wanted to trust the conviction in her voice. But the facts were the facts, and right now, they were painting a picture that defied all logic.

She leaned forward, replaying the footage once more. The man on the screen was a dead ringer for Mark Jennings, right down to the way he walked, the way he carried himself. But as she watched, Reyes couldn't shake the feeling that something was off. A flicker in the image, a glitch in the timestamp. It was subtle, almost imperceptible, but it was there.

THE HUSBAND

"I need to make a call," she said, straightening up. "Mrs. Jennings, please, try to stay calm. I promise you, we're doing everything we can to get to the bottom of this."

Rachel didn't respond, her gaze fixed on the screen, tears streaming down her face. Reyes hesitated for a moment, then turned and walked out of the room, her mind racing.

As she pulled out her phone, scrolling through her contacts, Reyes couldn't shake the sense of unease that had settled in the pit of her stomach. Something was wrong, very wrong, and she had a feeling that this was just the beginning.

She hit the call button, lifting the phone to her ear. "This is Detective Reyes. I need you to do something for me. Pull up everything we have on Mark Jennings. Employment history, travel records, everything. And see if you can find any connection to Kiev."

She paused, listening to the response on the other end of the line. "I don't know what's going on here," she said, her voice low and urgent. "But I have a feeling we're dealing with something a lot bigger than a simple case of mistaken identity."

The Phoenix sun beat down mercilessly as Reyes stepped out of her car, the heat rising in shimmering waves from the asphalt. She squinted against the glare, making her way towards the small cluster of witnesses gathered outside the convenience store.

"This is bullshit," a heavyset man in a sweat-stained t-shirt spat, his face flushed with anger. "We've been over this a hundred times already. What more do you want from us?"

Reyes held up her hands, her voice calm and even. "I understand your frustration, sir. But we have to be thorough. There are... inconsistencies that we need to address."

"Inconsistencies?" a woman with a tight blonde ponytail scoffed. "What's so hard to understand? We saw the guy, plain as day. He was right here, not even a week ago."

Reyes nodded, her eyes scanning the faces of the witnesses. They were all so certain, so unwavering in their accounts. But how could that be, when Mark Jennings was sitting in an interrogation room a thousand miles away?

"Look," she said, her voice low and urgent. "I know this seems straightforward to you. But we have evidence that suggests Mr. Jennings was in another country at the time you claim to have seen him. We're just trying to make sense of it all."

The witnesses exchanged incredulous glances, their frustration palpable. "Another country?" the heavyset man scoffed. "That's impossible. He was here, in the flesh. You think we're all just making this up?"

Reyes shook her head, her mind racing. She couldn't shake the feeling that there was something more at play here, something sinister lurking just beneath the surface.

"No one's accusing you of lying," she said, her voice firm. "But we have to consider all the evidence. And right now, that evidence is pointing us in a very different direction."

The witnesses fell silent, their anger giving way to confusion and unease. Reyes could see the doubt creeping into their eyes, the first cracks in their unwavering certainty.

She glanced down at her watch, her jaw tightening. She needed to get back to Austin, to confront Mark with the Kiev footage. She had a feeling that his reaction would be the key to unraveling this whole twisted mess.

"Thank you for your time," she said, turning to leave. "We'll be in touch if we have any further questions."

As she walked back to her car, Reyes couldn't shake the sense of dread that had settled in the pit of her stomach. She had a feeling that this case was about to take a turn for the surreal, and she wasn't sure if she was ready for what lay ahead.

THE HUSBAND

The interrogation room was cold and sterile, the fluorescent lights casting harsh shadows across Mark's face. He looked haggard and exhausted, his eyes bloodshot and ringed with dark circles.

Reyes sat across from him, the Kiev footage queued up on her laptop. She studied his face, searching for any flicker of recognition, any hint of guilt.

"I'm going to show you something," she said, her voice level and controlled. "And I need you to be completely honest with me about what you see."

Mark nodded, his eyes wary. "Of course. I've been nothing but honest with you from the start."

Reyes hit play, the grainy footage filling the screen. She watched Mark's face closely, her heart pounding in her chest.

At first, there was no reaction. But as the video played on, as the man in the footage turned to face the camera, Mark's eyes widened in shock and disbelief.

"What the fuck?" he whispered, his voice hoarse. "That's... that's me. But I swear to God, I've never been to Ukraine. This is impossible."

Reyes leaned forward, her eyes locked on Mark's. "Impossible or not, that's you in the video. And we have witnesses in Phoenix who swear they saw you there, just days ago. So you better start explaining, and fast."

Mark shook his head, his face pale and drawn. "I can't explain it," he said, his voice trembling. "I don't know what's going on. But I swear to you, I'm not lying. I didn't do this."

Reyes sat back in her chair, her mind racing. She believed him, God help her. But if Mark was telling the truth, then what the hell was going on? How could he be in three places at once?

She stood up abruptly, the chair scraping against the concrete floor. "I need a minute," she said, her voice tight. "Don't go anywhere."

As she stepped out of the room, Reyes leaned against the wall, her heart pounding. She had a feeling she was standing on the edge of something big, something that would change everything she thought she knew about the world.

And as she stared at the closed door of the interrogation room, she couldn't shake the sense that she was about to step into a nightmare from which there was no waking up.

The door to the station burst open, and Rachel Jennings stormed in, her eyes wild with desperation. She spotted Reyes and marched over, her hands clenched into fists at her sides.

"Detective Reyes," she said, her voice shaking with emotion. "You have to believe me. That man in there, he's not my husband. I don't know how, but someone is setting him up."

Reyes held up her hands, trying to calm the distraught woman. "Mrs. Jennings, I understand this is a difficult situation, but we have to follow the evidence-"

"Screw the evidence!" Rachel shouted, her face flushed with anger. "I know my husband. I know he didn't do this. And if you won't help him, then I'll find someone who will."

She spun on her heel and stalked away, leaving Reyes staring after her, a sinking feeling in her gut. She knew she should go after Rachel, try to reason with her, but her feet felt rooted to the spot.

Instead, she turned and walked back into the interrogation room, where Mark sat with his head in his hands. He looked up as she entered, his eyes red-rimmed and haunted.

"My wife," he said, his voice barely above a whisper. "Is she okay?"

Reyes hesitated, then sat down across from him. "She's upset," she said carefully. "But she believes in you. And so do I."

Mark's eyes widened in surprise. "You do?"

Reyes nodded, her jaw tight. "I don't know what's going on here, but I know there's more to this than meets the eye. And I'm going to find out what it is, no matter what it takes."

THE HUSBAND

She leaned forward, her gaze intense. "But I need you to be straight with me, Mark. Is there anything, anything at all, that you're not telling me?"

Mark hesitated, then shook his head. "No," he said, his voice firm. "I've told you everything I know."

Reyes sat back, her mind whirling with possibilities. Twins? Clones? Some kind of elaborate hoax? Each explanation seemed more far-fetched than the last.

But one thing was clear: she couldn't rest until she got to the bottom of this. Even if it meant going up against her own department, her own instincts.

She stood up, her shoulders squared with determination. "Sit tight," she told Mark. "I'm going to get to the bottom of this, I promise you."

As she walked out of the room, Reyes couldn't shake the feeling that she was walking into a labyrinth of lies and deception, one that would test her skills and her sanity to the limit.

But she was ready for the challenge. And God help anyone who stood in her way.

The conference room was filled with a palpable tension as Reyes stood before her superiors, the evidence spread out on the table before her. She could feel their skepticism, their dismissive glances boring into her as she outlined the case's complexities.

"Let me get this straight," Captain Jameson said, his voice dripping with condescension. "You're telling us that Mark Jennings, a man currently in our custody, was somehow also seen in Phoenix and Kiev at the same time?"

Reyes met his gaze unflinchingly. "I know how it sounds, sir. But the evidence is undeniable. We have multiple eyewitness accounts and CCTV footage confirming his presence in both locations."

Detective Harrison scoffed. "Come on, Reyes. You can't seriously believe this. It's obviously some kind of hoax, or maybe the guy has a twin he never told anyone about."

Reyes shook her head. "I've considered those possibilities, but the facts just don't add up. Mark Jennings has no known twin, and the logistics of staging such an elaborate hoax are almost impossible."

The room fell silent for a moment, the weight of her words hanging in the air. Finally, Captain Jameson spoke, his tone measured but firm.

"Detective Reyes, I understand your dedication to this case. But we can't chase after every wild theory that comes our way. Unless you have concrete proof, we have to proceed based on the evidence we have."

Reyes felt a surge of frustration, but she kept her voice steady. "With all due respect, sir, I believe this is the evidence we have. And I intend to follow it, wherever it leads."

The captain's eyes narrowed. "Be careful, Reyes. Don't let your obsession with this case cloud your judgment. We have a responsibility to the public, to close cases and bring criminals to justice."

Reyes met his gaze unflinchingly. "And that's exactly what I intend to do, sir. Even if it means going against the grain."

As the meeting adjourned, Reyes could feel the eyes of her colleagues on her back, their whispers following her out of the room. She knew they were questioning her judgment, her sanity even.

But she wouldn't let their doubts deter her. She had a mystery to solve, a truth to uncover. And she wouldn't rest until she had answers, no matter the cost.

Reyes stood in her dimly lit office, the only sound the distant hum of the bullpen beyond her door. She stared at the evidence board, a chaotic collage of photos, notes, and red string connecting the dots. Mark Jennings' face stared back at her from a dozen different angles, a silent plea for help.

She sighed, rubbing her temples. The meeting with her superiors had gone about as well as she'd expected. They thought she was losing it, chasing ghosts and conspiracy theories. But she knew, deep in her gut, that there was more to this case than met the eye.

THE HUSBAND 57

Her gaze drifted to the grainy still from the Kiev CCTV footage, the timestamp glaring at her like an accusation. How could Mark be in two places at once? It defied logic, reason, everything she'd ever known as a cop.

But the evidence was right there, staring her in the face. The witnesses in Phoenix, the ATM footage, Rachel's unwavering belief in her husband's innocence. It all pointed to something bigger, something she couldn't quite grasp.

Reyes leaned back against her desk, her mind racing. She knew she was risking everything by pursuing this case. Her reputation, her career, maybe even her sanity. But she couldn't let it go. She couldn't live with herself if she didn't see it through.

She straightened up, a new determination settling over her. Screw what the others thought. She was going to solve this mystery, even if it meant going rogue. She'd always trusted her instincts, and right now, they were screaming at her that there was more to this than met the eye.

Reyes turned back to the evidence board, her eyes scanning the sea of information. Somewhere in this mess was the key to unlocking the truth. And she wouldn't rest until she found it, no matter where it led her.

She took a deep breath, feeling the weight of the case settling on her shoulders. It was going to be a long night. But Samantha Reyes had never been one to back down from a challenge. And this, she knew, was the biggest challenge of her career.

With a final glance at Mark Jennings' haunted eyes, she grabbed her jacket and headed for the door. The game was on, and she was ready to play.

Reyes' feet hit the tarmac, her leather jacket flapping in the blast from the jet turbines. Kiev. Thousands of miles from home and umpteen time zones away from any semblance of normalcy. Her fingers itched for a cigarette to take the edge off.

She glanced at the photo in her hand. Mark Fucking Jennings. That weasley bastard had gone and vanished off the face of the earth, leaving behind nothing but a blurry ATM still and a dizzying trail of questions that ricocheted like bullets in Reyes' skull. Just what had he gotten mixed up in this time?

Shoving the photo back in her pocket, she strode toward the taxi stand, her compact frame cutting through the crowd like a stiletto. No time to waste. She had to get down to brass tacks with the local cops and start piecing this mind-fuck of a puzzle together.

The cab careened through Kiev's chaotic streets, a cacophony of blaring horns and revving engines. Vibrant street art flashed by in a blur - murals splashed with electric hues and bold, avant-garde forms. A stark contrast to the knot twisting in Reyes' gut.

She checked the photo again as the cab lurched to a stop. There was Jennings, caught in grainy black and white, hat pulled low on a hunched frame that screamed "don't look at me." Where the hell was he? What scheme was he neck deep in now? The questions multiplied like gremlins in water.

"Hey lady, you gettin' out or what?" The cabbie's gruff voice snapped Reyes back to the moment. She tossed some crumpled bills onto the front seat and swung out onto the curb, slamming the door with a satisfying thunk.

The police station loomed ahead, all imposing concrete and soulless architecture. Squaring her shoulders, Reyes marched toward the entrance, ready to go toe-to-toe with whatever awaited her inside. This crazy train was just leaving the station, and she'd be damned if she was gonna sit back and enjoy the ride.

Reyes shouldered through the police station's heavy doors, her boots echoing on the scuffed linoleum. The air reeked of stale coffee and bureaucracy. Cops milled about, some hunched over desks, others engaged in hushed conversations. All too busy to notice the whirlwind in their midst.

THE HUSBAND

She zeroed in on the front desk, manned by a bored-looking officer. "Special Agent Reyes, here to see Officer Ivanov." Her words were clipped, her tone brooking no argument.

The officer's eyes flicked up, taking in Reyes' no-nonsense stance and the fire in her gaze. He gestured toward a hallway. "Second door on the left."

Reyes gave a curt nod and strode off, her mind already ten steps ahead. She found the door ajar, a nameplate reading "Detective Sergei Ivanov" in both Ukrainian and English. She rapped her knuckles against the wood, the sound sharp in the buzzing fluorescent hum.

"Enter." The voice was gravelly, the accent thick.

She pushed inside, taking in the cramped office and the man behind the desk. Ivanov looked every bit the grizzled detective - salt-and-pepper hair, a face lined with experience, and eyes that had seen too much.

"Agent Reyes, I presume." Ivanov rose, extending a hand. "I've been expecting you."

Reyes gripped his hand firmly. "Glad to hear it. I'm not here to waste time, so let's cut to the chase. The ATM footage, the bank account - what do you know?"

Ivanov leaned back, a wry smile playing at the corners of his mouth. "Straight to the point. I like that." He pulled a file from his desk drawer and tossed it across to Reyes. "Everything we have so far. The address is in there."

Reyes flipped through the file, her eyes scanning the pages. An address jumped out at her, and she snapped the folder shut. "Then what are we waiting for? Let's go see what secrets this place holds."

Ivanov grabbed his coat, and they set off, the thrum of anticipation pulsing between them. Reyes' mind raced as they navigated the labyrinthine streets, the car's engine humming beneath the din of the city. Each turn brought them closer to the truth, but the dread in her gut only grew.

The apartment building was nondescript, just another face in the crowd. But as Reyes stepped out of the car, the weight of the unknown pressed down on her. She exchanged a glance with Ivanov, a silent acknowledgment of the darkness they were about to unravel.

Together, they approached the building, ready to confront whatever twisted secrets lay hidden behind its walls. The game was on, and Reyes was determined to come out on top, no matter the cost.

The stairs groaned beneath their feet, each step a protest against their intrusion. Dust hung thick in the air, catching in Reyes' throat as they ascended. She counted the doors, her heart pounding in time with their footfalls.

At last, they reached the apartment. Reyes raised her fist, poised to knock, but hesitated. The weight of possibility hung heavy in the air. What if Mark or Irina answered? What then?

She steeled herself and rapped sharply on the door, the sound echoing in the hollow silence of the hallway. Seconds ticked by, each one an eternity. No answer.

Ivanov stepped forward, his face set in grim determination. "Looks like we're doing this the hard way."

He drew a set of picks from his pocket and set to work on the lock, his hands moving with practiced precision. Reyes watched, her breath caught in her throat, as the lock clicked open.

The door swung inward, revealing a dimly lit apartment. They stepped inside, the floorboards creaking beneath their weight. And then Reyes saw it.

The walls were covered in a mad scrawl of symbols and equations, a chaotic tapestry of secrets. It was like stumbling into the fever dream of a mad scientist, a glimpse into a mind unhinged.

"What the hell is all this?" Ivanov muttered, his eyes wide.

Reyes moved closer, her fingertips tracing the strange markings. "I don't know, but I have a feeling it's the key to everything."

THE HUSBAND

She pulled out her phone and began snapping photos, determined to unravel the mystery. Each symbol seemed to mock her, a taunting reminder of how little she truly understood.

But Reyes was not one to back down from a challenge. She would decipher this code, no matter the cost. The truth was here, hidden in the mad scribbles of a fractured mind.

And she would not rest until she dragged it kicking and screaming into the light.

As Reyes lost herself in the cryptic symbols, a voice cut through the silence like a knife.

"Що ти тут робиш?"

Reyes spun around, her heart racing. An elderly woman stood in the doorway, her weathered face etched with a mixture of fear and curiosity.

Ivanov stepped forward, his hands raised in a placating gesture. He spoke in rapid Ukrainian, his words a soothing balm to the woman's frayed nerves.

But Reyes barely registered their exchange. Her attention was drawn back to the walls, to the secrets they held. She moved from one symbol to the next, her mind whirring with possibilities.

What did they mean? Were they a code, a message from beyond the grave? Or were they the ramblings of a mind lost to madness?

Reyes didn't know, but she was determined to find out. She would peel back the layers of this mystery, one maddening symbol at a time.

The elderly woman's voice grew more insistent, her words laced with a growing hysteria. Ivanov tried to calm her, but Reyes could see the strain on his face.

They were running out of time. The walls were closing in, the symbols taunting her with their secrets.

Reyes took one last photo, her finger hovering over the capture button. And then she saw it.

A pattern, a glimmer of meaning in the chaos. It was there, just out of reach, dancing on the edges of her understanding.

She turned to Ivanov, her eyes wide with realization. "We need to go. Now."

He nodded, his jaw clenched. They made their apologies to the elderly woman and slipped out of the apartment, the weight of their discovery heavy on their shoulders.

The symbols burned in Reyes' mind, a silent promise of the truth to come. She would unravel this mystery, one maddening piece at a time.

And God help anyone who stood in her way.

As they hurried down the creaky stairs, Reyes' mind raced with the implications of the neighbor's revelation. Multiple Marks? What the hell was going on here?

Ivanov's brow furrowed as he processed the information. "This case keeps getting stranger by the minute. What do you make of it, Reyes?"

Reyes shook her head, a wry smile playing on her lips. "I don't know what to think anymore. Clones? Secret twins? A glitch in the fucking Matrix? Your guess is as good as mine."

Ivanov chuckled darkly. "Well, whatever it is, we better figure it out fast. I've got a feeling this is just the tip of the iceberg."

Reyes nodded, her eyes scanning the street as they emerged from the building. The city bustled around them, oblivious to the mind-bending mystery unfolding in their midst.

She couldn't shake the unease that crept up her spine, the feeling that they were being watched. The idea of multiple Marks sent a shiver through her, a twisted echo of the man she thought she knew.

Reyes climbed into the car, her mind whirring with possibilities. She needed answers, and she needed them now. But where to start? The symbols in the apartment? The bank account? The neighbor's story?

She closed her eyes, trying to focus. The pieces were there, scattered and disjointed, waiting to be assembled. She just needed to find the right angle, the right thread to pull.

THE HUSBAND

Ivanov's voice broke through her thoughts. "Where to now, Reyes? Back to the station?"

Reyes shook her head, a newfound determination settling over her. "No. We need to find Irina. She's the key to all of this. I can feel it."

Ivanov nodded, his eyes meeting hers in the rearview mirror. "You got it, boss. Let's track her down and get some goddamn answers."

Reyes smiled grimly, her hand tightening on the door handle. They were close, she could feel it. Close to the truth, close to the heart of this twisted mystery.

And when they found it, there would be hell to pay.

The car sped through the streets of Kiev, Reyes' mind racing faster than the engine. She couldn't shake the feeling that they were on the precipice of something big, something that would blow this case wide open.

She glanced at the photos on her phone, the strange symbols and equations seared into her memory. What did they mean? What secrets did they hold?

Ivanov's voice cut through her thoughts. "You know, in all my years on the force, I've never seen anything like this. Multiple doppelgangers, cryptic symbols, international intrigue... it's like something out of a damn spy novel."

Reyes snorted. "Yeah, well, let's just hope it doesn't end with us face down in a ditch somewhere."

Ivanov chuckled darkly. "Amen to that."

The car pulled up to the police station, and Reyes and Ivanov made their way inside. The building buzzed with activity, a hive of cops and criminals, paperwork and procedure.

But Reyes couldn't focus on any of it. Her mind was stuck on those symbols, on the mystery of Mark Jennings and his legion of lookalikes.

She found an empty conference room and spread out the photos, her eyes scanning each one for clues. But the more she looked, the more frustrated she became.

"Damn it," she muttered, running a hand through her hair. "It's like trying to solve a puzzle with half the pieces missing."

Ivanov leaned against the doorframe, his arms crossed. "Maybe we're looking at this the wrong way. Maybe the symbols aren't the key. Maybe it's the people behind them."

Reyes looked up, her eyes narrowing. "Irina."

Ivanov nodded. "Exactly. We need to find her, see what she knows. And we need to do it fast, before this whole thing spirals out of control."

Reyes stood up, a new sense of purpose coursing through her. "Then let's get to work. Let's find Irina and get some answers, once and for all."

She strode out of the conference room, Ivanov hot on her heels. The weight of the mystery still pressed down on her, but now it felt like a challenge, not a burden.

And Reyes Abadi never backed down from a challenge.

The harsh glow of the computer screen illuminated Reyes' face as her fingers flew across the keyboard. She cross-referenced the symbols with every database she could think of: ancient languages, modern ciphers, even obscure academic journals.

But each search ended in a frustrating dead end.

Ivanov sat across from her, his own eyes glued to a screen. "Anything?" he asked, his voice gruff with fatigue.

Reyes shook her head. "Nothing. It's like these symbols don't even exist."

She leaned back in her chair, rubbing her temples. The fluorescent lights of the police station felt harsh and unforgiving, a stark contrast to the enigmatic darkness of the apartment.

"We're missing something," she said, more to herself than to Ivanov. "Something obvious, something right in front of our faces."

Ivanov grunted in agreement. "Maybe we need a fresh set of eyes. Someone who thinks outside the box."

THE HUSBAND

Reyes' mind flashed to Professor Novak, the eccentric academic who had first tipped her off about the symbols. He was a long shot, but at this point, any lead was better than no lead.

She pulled out her phone and dialed his number, her heart racing as it rang.

"Professor Novak," she said when he finally answered. "It's Reyes Abadi. I need your help."

There was a long pause on the other end of the line. Then, in a voice heavy with both excitement and trepidation, Novak spoke.

"I was wondering when you'd call. I think I know what those symbols mean. But you're not going to like it."

Reyes gripped the phone tighter, her knuckles turning white. "Tell me."

As Novak began to explain, Reyes felt a chill run down her spine. The pieces of the puzzle were finally falling into place, but the picture they formed was more terrifying than she ever could have imagined.

She glanced at Ivanov, who was watching her with a mix of curiosity and concern. "We need to move," she said, her voice harsh with urgency. "Now."

Ivanov didn't hesitate. He grabbed his coat and followed Reyes out the door, into the cold Kiev night.

The game had changed. And Reyes was determined to win.

Reyes and Ivanov sped through the darkened streets of Kiev, the car's headlights cutting through the gloom. Reyes' mind raced with the information Novak had shared, the implications sending a cold sweat down her back.

"Where the hell are we going?" Ivanov asked, his eyes flicking between the road and Reyes.

"The university," Reyes replied, her voice tight. "Novak's lab. He said he has something to show us."

Ivanov grunted, pushing the accelerator to the floor. "This better be good."

Reyes didn't respond, her thoughts consumed by the twisted web she found herself entangled in. The symbols, the multiple Marks, Irina's disappearance - it all pointed to something far more sinister than she had ever imagined.

They screeched to a halt outside the university, the tires leaving black marks on the asphalt. Reyes leapt from the car, Ivanov close on her heels, as they raced towards Novak's lab.

The lab was dark, save for a single light illuminating a cluttered desk. Novak sat hunched over a microscope, his face pale and drawn.

"Professor," Reyes called out, her voice echoing in the empty room.

Novak looked up, his eyes wide behind his glasses. "You came."

"What is this about?" Ivanov demanded, his hand resting on his holster.

Novak stood, his hands shaking as he reached for a folder on his desk. "The symbols," he said, his voice trembling. "I've seen them before."

Reyes snatched the folder from his hands, her eyes scanning the contents. Her heart stopped as she realized what she was looking at.

"Project Gemini," she whispered, her voice barely audible.

Novak nodded, his face grim. "A secret Soviet experiment from the Cold War. They were trying to create the perfect soldier, one who could be in multiple places at once."

Ivanov scoffed. "That's impossible."

"Is it?" Reyes asked, her mind spinning with the implications. "The multiple Marks, the strange behavior - what if they succeeded?"

Novak ran a hand through his thinning hair. "I thought it was just a myth, a cautionary tale. But the symbols in that apartment - they match the ones in these files."

Reyes felt a chill run down her spine. "So what are we dealing with here? Clones? Doppelgangers?"

"Something far worse," Novak replied, his voice barely a whisper. "Something that could change the course of history."

THE HUSBAND

Reyes and Ivanov exchanged a glance, the weight of Novak's words hanging heavy in the air.

They were no longer just chasing a missing person. They were unraveling a decades-old conspiracy, one that threatened to upend everything they thought they knew.

And at the center of it all was Mark Jennings, a man who might not even be a man at all.

The hotel room felt like a pressure cooker, the walls closing in as Reyes stared at the cryptic symbols on her phone. Each equation taunted her, a secret language she couldn't crack. She tossed the phone on the bed and paced the room, her mind spinning like a roulette wheel.

"What the fuck am I missing?" she muttered, running a hand through her disheveled hair. The symbols burned into her retinas, refusing to reveal their secrets.

Reyes grabbed a beer from the mini-fridge and popped the cap, taking a long swig. The cool liquid did little to quench the fire in her brain. She collapsed into the desk chair, her eyes drawn back to the phone like a moth to a flame.

"Think, Reyes, think," she growled, zooming in on one particularly complex equation. The numbers and symbols blurred together, a Rorschach test of confusion.

She closed her eyes, trying to clear her mind. Irina's face flashed behind her eyelids, a reminder of the human element at stake. Reyes couldn't shake the feeling that Irina held a piece of the puzzle, a key to unlocking the mystery.

"I need a fucking break," Reyes sighed, pushing away from the desk. She grabbed her jacket and headed for the door, desperate for some fresh air and a change of scenery.

As she stepped into the hallway, Reyes felt the weight of the case on her shoulders. The symbols, the multiple Marks, the strange behavior -

it all pointed to something bigger than she could imagine. But Reyes was never one to back down from a challenge.

"I'll figure this out," she vowed, her jaw set with determination. "Even if it kills me."

With that, Reyes strode down the hallway, ready to face whatever twists and turns the case would throw her way. The night was young, and so was the investigation.

Detective Samantha Reyes barged into the cluttered office of Dr. Alan Mercer without knocking. Stacks of physics journals and coffee-stained notebooks teetered precariously on the desk. The renowned quantum physicist looked up from his computer, startled.

Reyes fixed him with a steely gaze. "Dr. Mercer, I need answers and I'm not leaving until I get them."

Mercer leaned back in his chair, eyebrow raised. "Detective Reyes, is it? To what do I owe the pleasure?"

She tossed a manila folder on his desk, photos and reports spilling out. "Mark Jennings. Wanted for a string of bizarre crimes that defy explanation. Witnesses put him in two places at once, locked rooms broken into without a trace, getaway cars vanishing into thin air."

"Sounds like you've been reading too many science fiction novels, Detective." Mercer leafed through the file, his skepticism plain.

Reyes pressed on, undeterred. "Except it's all true. And the only connection is quantum physics - your area of expertise. So cut the crap and level with me, doc."

"You can't possibly think Jennings is using quantum mechanics to pull off some kind of magic trick?"

"You tell me. Bilocation, quantum tunneling, teleportation - any of this ringing a bell?" She watched his face closely.

Mercer sighed, running a hand through his graying hair. "Those are theoretical concepts, Detective. Science fiction. They have no place in reality."

THE HUSBAND 69

Bullshit, Reyes thought. This smug prick knows more than he's letting on.

"Look, I don't have time for a physics lesson," she snapped. "But I know Jennings is connected to your research somehow. And I'm going to find out what you're hiding, with or without your cooperation."

Reyes held his gaze, unflinching. She'd faced down psychopaths and killers - one arrogant academic wasn't about to stand in her way. Not when she was this close to the truth.

No matter how crazy it sounded, even to her.

Mercer leaned back in his chair, an infuriating smirk playing on his lips. "I admire your tenacity, Detective, but I'm afraid you're barking up the wrong tree. My research is purely theoretical, with no practical applications. Certainly nothing that could explain your suspect's alleged... abilities."

Reyes slammed her hand on the desk, scattering papers. "Dammit, Mercer! I have evidence that says otherwise. Witnesses who swear they saw Jennings in two places at once. Security footage that shows him disappearing into thin air."

She pulled out a grainy photograph from the file and shoved it under his nose. "Explain this. Jennings, caught on camera in his cell, and simultaneously robbing a bank across town. Timestamped and verified."

Mercer's eyes widened slightly, but he quickly schooled his features. "Clever forgery, perhaps? Or a twin brother you're unaware of?" His tone dripped with condescension.

Reyes gritted her teeth, fighting the urge to wipe that smug look off his face. "We've ruled out all the logical explanations. Which leaves us with the impossible."

She leaned in closer, her voice low and intense. "I think you know exactly how Jennings is doing this. And I think it has everything to do with your 'theoretical' research."

Mercer shifted in his seat, a flicker of unease crossing his features. "I'm sorry, Detective, but I really can't help you. Even if what you're suggesting were possible - and I'm not saying it is - I have no idea how Jennings could be exploiting quantum phenomena."

Reyes studied him, looking for the lie. There was something there, a hint of doubt in his eyes. He knew more than he was letting on, but pushing him further now would be futile.

She gathered up the files, her mouth set in a determined line. "This isn't over, Mercer. I'll find the truth, with or without you."

As she turned to leave, Mercer called out, "Detective, wait."

Reyes paused, looking back over her shoulder.

"Be careful," he said, his voice oddly sincere. "If Jennings is somehow manipulating quantum reality... you're treading in dangerous waters. There's no telling what he's capable of, or what the consequences might be."

A chill ran down Reyes's spine, but she refused to show it. With a curt nod, she strode out of the office, her mind already racing ahead to her next move.

The holding cells at the Austin police station were a stark contrast to the cluttered chaos of Dr. Mercer's office. Fluorescent lights buzzed overhead, casting a sickly glow on the concrete walls. The air was thick with the stench of sweat and desperation.

In the far cell, Mark Jennings paced like a caged animal, his movements erratic and agitated. His eyes darted around the confined space, never settling on any one thing for more than a second. The two guards stationed outside his cell watched him with a mix of boredom and unease.

"Guy's been like that for hours," the older guard muttered, taking a sip of his coffee. "You'd think he'd tire himself out eventually."

The younger guard shrugged. "Maybe he's tweaking. Wouldn't be the first junkie to lose his shit in here."

THE HUSBAND

Inside the cell, Jennings' mind raced with fragmented thoughts and memories. The walls seemed to pulse and warp around him, reality bending at the seams. He could feel it happening again, the inexplicable pull of something beyond his understanding.

"No, no, no," he mumbled, pressing his palms against his temples. "Not again. Not here."

But the force was relentless, tugging at the very fabric of his being. He could feel his molecules vibrating, his atoms splitting apart and reforming in impossible ways. The sensation was both terrifying and exhilarating, a rush of power and chaos that threatened to consume him.

The guards remained oblivious, their attention focused on their idle conversation. They didn't notice the way the air around Jennings began to shimmer and distort, like heat rising off a desert highway.

And then, in a flash of blinding light, Mark Jennings vanished. One moment he was there, a solid presence of flesh and bone, and the next he was simply gone, leaving behind an empty cell and a deafening silence.

The older guard's coffee mug slipped from his fingers, shattering on the concrete floor. The sound was like a gunshot in the stillness, jolting them both from their stupor.

"What the fuck?" the younger guard breathed, his eyes wide with disbelief. "Where'd he go?"

But there were no answers, only the echoing absence where Mark Jennings had once stood. The guards stared at each other, their faces mirroring the same mix of shock and incomprehension.

In that moment, they knew that everything had changed. The impossible had become real, and the world would never be the same again.

The flickering glow of the security monitors cast an eerie blue light across Reyes's face as she leaned in, her eyes narrowed in disbelief. She hit the rewind button, watching as the impossible moment played out again and again.

"This can't be real," Detective Thompson muttered, his voice tinged with awe. "People don't just... disappear."

Reyes shook her head, her mind racing. "But there it is, right in front of us. One second he's there, and the next..."

She trailed off, unable to find the words. The footage was undeniable, a stark reminder that the world she thought she knew was just a fragile illusion.

"What do we do now?" Thompson asked, his gaze locked on the screen. "How do we even begin to explain this?"

Reyes felt a chill run down her spine, a primal fear that she couldn't quite shake. If Mark Jennings could vanish into thin air, what other impossibilities were waiting in the shadows?

"We need answers," she said, her voice steady despite the tremor in her hands. "We need to find out what the hell is going on here."

But even as the words left her mouth, Reyes knew that the truth might be more than she was ready to handle. The implications of what she'd just witnessed were staggering, a paradigm shift that threatened to upend everything she thought she knew.

Could this be connected to the other strange events surrounding Mark Jennings? The thought whispered through her mind, insidious and unsettling. *If he can do this, what else is he capable of?*

Reyes pushed herself back from the desk, her chair scraping against the linoleum. She needed to move, to do something, anything to quiet the rising panic in her chest.

"I want every scrap of information we have on Jennings," she barked, her voice echoing in the cramped room. "Every witness statement, every piece of evidence. We're going to tear this case apart until we find some goddamn answers."

Thompson nodded, his expression grim. "I'm on it, boss. But what if we don't like what we find?"

Reyes met his gaze, her eyes hard with determination. "Then we keep digging until we do. We're not going to let this one go, no matter where it leads us."

And with that, she strode from the room, her mind already churning with the possibilities. She knew she was stepping into uncharted territory, but there was no turning back now. The truth was out there, and she would stop at nothing to find it.

The conference room felt claustrophobic, the air thick with tension as Reyes faced her superiors. Captain Davis leaned back in his chair, his expression a mix of skepticism and concern. "Detective Reyes, I've been hearing some troubling reports about your investigation."

Reyes met his gaze unflinchingly. "Sir, I'm following the evidence. The footage from the holding cell is clear. Mark Jennings vanished into thin air."

Davis sighed, rubbing his temples. "Reyes, you're talking about the impossible. People don't just disappear."

"With all due respect, Captain, that's exactly what happened." Reyes leaned forward, her hands planted firmly on the table. "I know it sounds crazy, but we have video proof."

Lieutenant Chen spoke up, her tone condescending. "Detective, have you considered that perhaps the stress of this case is getting to you? It wouldn't be the first time an officer's judgment was clouded by emotional involvement."

Anger flared in Reyes's chest, but she tamped it down. *Stay focused. Don't let them dismiss you.* "I'm not imagining things, Lieutenant. The evidence is right there in front of us."

Davis held up a hand, silencing Chen's retort. "Let's say, for the sake of argument, that what you're claiming is true. What do you propose we do about it? We can't exactly put out an APB on a man who can teleport."

Reyes took a deep breath, choosing her words carefully. "We need to bring in experts, people who can help us understand what we're dealing with. Quantum physicists, parapsychologists, anyone who might have insight into how this could be possible."

Chen scoffed. "You want us to bring in a bunch of crackpots and pseudoscientists? This is a police investigation, not a sci-fi convention."

Ignore her. Stay on message. "The evidence speaks for itself, even if it defies conventional understanding. We have a responsibility to pursue the truth, no matter where it leads."

Davis studied her for a long moment, his expression unreadable. "You're treading on thin ice, Detective. This department has a reputation to uphold."

Reyes met his gaze squarely. "With all due respect, sir, our reputation should be based on our commitment to the truth, not our ability to sweep the inexplicable under the rug."

You're pushing it, Reyes. Tone it down. She took a breath, forcing herself to soften her tone. "I know I'm asking a lot, but I wouldn't be here if I didn't believe in this case. Give me a chance to prove it. That's all I'm asking."

Davis exchanged a glance with Chen, a silent conversation passing between them. Finally, he sighed. "You have 48 hours, Reyes. If you can't provide concrete evidence to support your claims, I'm pulling you off this case. Understood?"

Reyes nodded, relief flooding through her. "Understood, sir. Thank you."

As she left the conference room, Reyes could feel the weight of their skepticism bearing down on her. *They think you're losing it, Reyes. Prove them wrong.*

She squared her shoulders, her resolve hardening. She had 48 hours to unravel the mystery of Mark Jennings, and she wasn't going to waste a single second.

Reyes strode through the bustling bullpen, her mind racing with possibilities. She could feel the curious stares of her colleagues, their

THE HUSBAND

whispers trailing behind her like wisps of smoke. *Let them talk. You've got work to do.*

She reached her desk, sinking into her chair with a heavy sigh. The scattered files and half-empty coffee cups were a testament to the long hours she'd already poured into this case. *And it's only just beginning.*

Reyes pulled out her notebook, flipping through the pages of scrawled theories and hastily sketched diagrams. There had to be a connection, a thread that tied it all together. *Think, Reyes. What are you missing?*

Her eyes landed on a name, scribbled in the margin of one of the pages. Dr. Evelyn Thorne, a renowned expert in quantum entanglement. Reyes had come across her work during her initial research, but had dismissed it as too far-fetched. *But what if it's not? What if there's something to it after all?*

She grabbed her phone, dialing the number listed on Dr. Thorne's faculty page. The call connected after two rings, a crisp British accent answering on the other end.

"Dr. Thorne speaking. How may I assist you?"

Reyes took a breath, steeling herself. "Dr. Thorne, this is Detective Samantha Reyes with the Austin Police Department. I'm working on a case that I believe may have a connection to your research. I was hoping we could meet to discuss it further."

There was a pause on the other end, a moment of consideration. "I see. And what exactly is the nature of this case, Detective?"

Here goes nothing. "It involves a suspect who appears to have the ability to be in two places at once. I know it sounds impossible, but I have evidence that suggests otherwise."

Another pause, longer this time. *She thinks you're a lunatic. Great job, Reyes.*

But when Dr. Thorne spoke again, her tone was intrigued. "Very well, Detective. I'll clear my schedule for this afternoon. Shall we say 2 o'clock, my office at the university?"

Reyes felt a surge of hope, a flicker of validation. "2 o'clock. I'll be there. Thank you, Dr. Thorne."

As she hung up the phone, Reyes leaned back in her chair, a small smile tugging at the corners of her mouth. *Maybe, just maybe, you're not crazy after all.*

Reyes stood outside the precinct, the bustling sounds of the city a distant hum as she stared into the distance. The weight of the mystery hung heavy on her shoulders, a burden she carried alone. Her superiors' skepticism still rang in her ears, their dismissive tones and raised eyebrows etched into her memory.

Fuck 'em, she thought, her jaw set with determination. *They want concrete explanations? I'll give them concrete explanations. And then some.*

She reached into her pocket, fingers brushing against the cool metal of her car keys. The temptation to drive straight to Dr. Thorne's office, to unravel this impossible case, was almost overwhelming. But Reyes knew better than to rush in unprepared.

One step at a time, Samantha. One fucking step at a time.

She turned on her heel, striding back into the precinct with renewed purpose. The fluorescent lights flickered overhead, casting harsh shadows across the worn linoleum. Reyes navigated the maze of desks and filing cabinets, her mind already racing ahead to her next move.

Jennings' file. Need to review it again. There's got to be something I missed, some clue that ties this all together.

She reached her desk, the surface cluttered with papers and empty coffee cups. Reyes sank into her chair, the leather creaking beneath her weight. She flipped open the file, her eyes scanning the pages with laser focus.

Quantum physics. Bilocation. Teleportation. It's all here, hidden between the lines. Just waiting for someone to connect the dots.

THE HUSBAND

Reyes leaned back, her gaze drifting to the window. The city stretched out before her, a sprawling labyrinth of secrets and lies. She knew, with a bone-deep certainty, that the truth was out there. Waiting to be uncovered.

And I'm going to find it. Even if it kills me.

With a final glance at the file, Reyes pushed herself to her feet. She had work to do, leads to chase, a mystery to solve. The weight of it all still hung heavy, but her resolve was unshaken.

Time to dive deeper into the unknown.

Detective Samantha Reyes slumped at her desk, phone wedged between her ear and shoulder as she shuffled through the chaos of case files littering her office. "Come on, Anderson, there's gotta be something juicy from his college days," she pressed, her free hand rubbing at the knot of tension forming between her brows. "A guy like Jennings doesn't just vanish without a trace."

The voice on the other end of the line crackled with hesitation. "Look, Samantha, I've dug through every record we have on the guy. Dean's list, research grants, glowing recommendations from the faculty. He was a damn prodigy, but squeaky clean as far as I can tell."

"Shit." Reyes dropped the phone into its cradle with more force than necessary. Her gut told her there was more to the story, a thread she hadn't pulled hard enough. She reached for the thick manila folder balanced precariously on a stack of papers, the name "Mark Jennings" emblazoned across the tab in bold black marker.

Flipping it open, she skimmed the pages, her eyes catching on familiar details. Graduated summa cum laude, IQ off the charts, groundbreaking work in quantum physics. Yadda, yadda. Then, a line that made her pause, brows knitting together.

"Subject experienced a sudden decline in academic performance during senior year, coinciding with the onset of erratic behavior and withdrawal from social circles." Reyes read aloud, her voice a low murmur in the empty room. "The hell happened to you, Jennings?"

She leaned back in her chair, the springs creaking under her weight. A rising star, burned out before he could even hit his prime. It was a familiar story, but something about it nagged at her. The missing piece that would make it all slot into place.

Reyes tossed the file back onto her desk, watching as it skidded across the surface before coming to rest against a half-empty coffee mug. She needed answers, and she sure as hell wasn't going to find them buried in some musty old records.

Time to rattle some cages, she thought, pushing herself up from her chair with a determined set to her jaw. Starting with the man himself. Mark Jennings couldn't hide forever. And Samantha Reyes? She was just the bloodhound to sniff him out.

The scene cut to a bustling science fair, the air electric with the hum of young minds at work. Amid the sea of trifold boards and bubbling beakers, one exhibit stood out like a beacon. A gangly teenage boy, all sharp elbows and sharper eyes, stood beside a contraption that looked like it belonged in a sci-fi flick.

"Particle accelerator," he announced, his voice cracking with the bravado of youth. "Built it myself."

The judges, a motley crew of tweed-clad professors and bored industry types, perked up at that. They swarmed the booth, peppering the kid with questions that he fielded with ease. His hands danced over the machine as he explained its inner workings, his face alight with the thrill of discovery.

"Remarkable," one judge breathed, jotting furious notes on his clipboard. "Simply remarkable."

The boy, Mark Jennings, just shrugged, a half-smile tugging at his lips. He wasn't in it for the praise. He was in it for the rush, the high of pushing the boundaries of what was possible.

But even then, there was a shadow behind his eyes. A flicker of something darker, lurking beneath the surface.

THE HUSBAND

The scene shifted, the colors bleeding away until Reyes was back in her office, the glow of her computer screen casting harsh shadows across her face. She was on a video call, the face of a grizzled old professor filling the screen.

"Mark Jennings," the man said, his voice tinged with a mix of admiration and regret. "Brilliant kid. Brilliant mind. But he was always wound too tight, you know?"

Reyes leaned forward, her elbows digging into the desk. "What do you mean?"

The professor sighed, rubbing a hand over his face. "The pressure. It gets to all of them, sooner or later. The prodigies. They burn too bright, too fast. And Mark? He was burning brighter than most."

"What happened?" Reyes pressed, her pulse quickening.

"He cracked," the professor said simply. "The stress, the expectations. It all came crashing down on him. One day he was on top of the world, the next..." He trailed off, his eyes distant. "He just couldn't handle it anymore."

Reyes sat back, her mind reeling. The pieces were starting to fall into place, but the picture they formed was far from pretty. Mark Jennings, the golden boy, the rising star. Broken by the very thing that made him special.

She glanced at the journal on her desk, its strange symbols seeming to mock her. What secrets did it hold? What demons had Mark Jennings been battling, all those years ago?

She needed to find out. Needed to unravel the mystery before it was too late. Because something told her that Mark Jennings' disappearance was just the tip of the iceberg. That there was something far darker, far more dangerous, lurking beneath the surface.

And Samantha Reyes? She was diving in headfirst, consequences be damned.

The café bustled with the lunchtime crowd, a cacophony of clinking cutlery and muted conversations. Rachel Jennings sat in a corner booth, her fingers tracing the edges of a worn photograph. Detective Reyes slid into the seat opposite her, the vinyl squeaking beneath her weight.

"Thanks for meeting me," Reyes said, her voice low. She nodded towards the photograph. "That them? Mark and his brother?"

Rachel's hand stilled, her eyes flicking up to meet Reyes'. "Yes. Mark and Michael. Twins, but you'd never know it to look at them."

Reyes leaned in, studying the image. Two boys, maybe ten years old, stood side by side. One grinned at the camera, all sunshine and mischief. The other looked away, his expression guarded, distant.

"Michael was different," Rachel murmured, her thumb brushing over the withdrawn boy's face. "Quieter. More intense. He and Mark, they had this... connection. Like they could read each other's thoughts."

Reyes' brow furrowed. "Had?"

Rachel's lips pressed into a thin line. She set the photograph down, her hands trembling slightly. "Michael died. When they were sixteen."

Reyes' breath caught. She hadn't seen that in the files. "What happened?"

"No one knows." Rachel's voice was barely a whisper. "He just... disappeared one day. They found his body a week later, in the woods behind their house."

Reyes' mind raced, the implications sinking in. "And Mark?"

Rachel's eyes glistened with unshed tears. "He was never the same. It was like... like a part of him died with Michael."

Reyes leaned back, her heart pounding. The missing piece of the puzzle, the key to unlocking Mark Jennings' past. His twin's death, the catalyst for his unraveling.

"Rachel," she said softly, reaching across the table to grasp the other woman's hand. "I know this is hard. But I need to know... do you think Mark's disappearance could be connected to Michael's death?"

Rachel's fingers tightened around Reyes', her knuckles white. "I don't know," she whispered, her voice cracking. "But I've always had

THE HUSBAND

this feeling... this awful, gnawing feeling that there was more to it. That Michael's death wasn't an accident."

Reyes nodded, her jaw clenching. She'd had hunches like that before, the kind that kept her up at night, chasing leads that others had long since abandoned.

"I'll find out," she promised, her voice fierce with determination. "I'll find out what happened to Michael. And I'll bring Mark home, Rachel. I swear it."

Rachel's lips trembled, a single tear spilling down her cheek. "Thank you," she breathed, her grip on Reyes' hand tightening. "Thank you."

Reyes held her gaze, a silent vow passing between them. She would get to the bottom of this, no matter the cost. She owed it to Rachel, to Mark.

And to the ghost of a boy, lost in the woods all those years ago.

The corkboard loomed before Reyes, a chaotic mosaic of Mark Jennings' life. Photos, newspaper clippings, scribbled notes - all connected by a web of red string, a scarlet spider's silk weaving through the years.

She stepped back, her eyes narrowed, searching for the pattern amidst the madness. There, in the center, the date circled in thick, black marker. The day the world had shattered for the Jennings twins.

"What the hell happened to you, Michael?" Reyes muttered, her finger tracing the string from the fateful date to a grainy photo of two boys, their grins identical, their arms slung around each other's shoulders.

She'd read the reports, the cold, clinical words that reduced a life to a series of facts. Michael Jennings, age 17. Cause of death: accidental drowning. Case closed.

But the reports didn't tell the whole story. They didn't speak of the strained relationship between the brothers, the resentment that had festered beneath the surface. They didn't mention the strange symbols that had adorned Michael's bedroom walls, the same ones that had been carved into the leather-bound journal in Mark's apartment.

Reyes' gut churned, a familiar unease settling in the pit of her stomach. There was more to this, she could feel it in her bones. And the answers, she knew, lay hidden in the Jennings' attic, buried beneath the dust and the memories.

She grabbed her keys, her jaw set with determination. It was time to dig deeper, to unearth the secrets that had lain dormant for far too long.

The drive to the Jennings' house was a blur, Reyes' mind whirring with possibilities. She barely registered the scenery flashing by, the suburbs giving way to winding, tree-lined streets.

Rachel was waiting on the porch when she arrived, her arms wrapped tightly around herself, as if to ward off a chill despite the warm, summer air.

"Detective Reyes," she greeted, her voice strained. "I didn't expect you so soon."

Reyes climbed the steps, her boots heavy on the weathered wood. "I need to see the attic, Rachel. I think there might be something there, something that could help us find Mark."

Rachel hesitated, her eyes darting to the front door, as if weighing the consequences of letting Reyes inside. But then, with a shaky exhale, she nodded.

"Okay," she said softly, her hand trembling as she reached for the doorknob. "But I haven't been up there in years. Not since..."

She trailed off, her voice catching on the unspoken name. Michael. The ghost that haunted them all.

Reyes placed a gentle hand on Rachel's shoulder, a silent gesture of support. "I know," she murmured. "But we have to try. For Mark's sake."

Rachel nodded, her jaw tightening with resolve. She pushed open the door, the hinges creaking in protest.

THE HUSBAND

"The attic's this way," she said, leading Reyes through the dimly lit foyer. "I just hope... I hope you find what you're looking for."

Reyes followed, her heart pounding in her chest. She hoped so too. Because if she didn't, if the answers she sought remained buried in the shadows...

She didn't want to think about what that would mean for Mark. Or for the family he'd left behind.

The attic stairs groaned beneath Reyes' feet, each step a chorus of creaks and whispers. She gripped the railing, her knuckles white in the dim light. Dust motes danced in the beam of her flashlight, swirling like ghostly apparitions.

"Christ," she muttered, her nose wrinkling at the musty scent. "Smells like my grandma's underwear drawer up here."

The air was thick and heavy, laden with the weight of forgotten memories. Reyes reached the top, her flashlight cutting through the gloom. Shadows lurched and sprawled, cast by the hulking shapes of boxes and furniture.

She moved deeper into the attic, her boots leaving imprints in the dust. The beam of her flashlight flitted from one box to the next, searching for anything that might hold a clue.

"C'mon, Mark," she whispered, her voice barely audible over the thrum of her own heartbeat. "Where'd you hide your secrets?"

Her fingers brushed against the edge of a box, the cardboard soft and yielding beneath her touch. She tugged it open, the contents spilling out in a cascade of childhood memorabilia. Faded photographs, tattered comic books, a rusted toy car.

And there, nestled amongst the detritus of Mark's past, a leather-bound journal. Reyes reached for it, her breath catching in her throat. The cover was etched with strange symbols, their meaning lost to time and dust.

"What the hell?" she murmured, running her fingers over the intricate designs. "What is this, some kind of code?"

She flipped open the journal, the pages crackling with age. The handwriting was a jagged scrawl, the ink faded to a dull brown. But it was the drawings that caught her eye, sketches of machines and diagrams that made no sense.

Reyes' heart hammered in her chest, a sense of unease prickling at the back of her neck. She couldn't shake the feeling that she was on the cusp of something big, something that would change everything.

"What were you into, Mark?" she whispered, her eyes scanning the pages. "What kind of mess did you get yourself mixed up in?"

As Reyes delved deeper into the journal, a chill crept down her spine. The symbols, the diagrams - they were identical to the ones she'd seen in the Kiev apartment. The very same apartment where Mark had last been seen alive.

"Son of a bitch," she breathed, her mind racing with the implications. "It's all connected. But how?"

She flipped through the pages with trembling fingers, her eyes darting from one cryptic entry to the next. Equations, formulas, sketches of machines that looked like something out of a science fiction novel. And woven throughout, a narrative of obsession and desperation.

Reyes paused on a page marked with a date from five years ago, a single sentence scrawled in Mark's frantic hand: "I have to stop him before it's too late."

"Stop who?" Reyes muttered, her brow furrowed in concentration. "Your brother? Or someone else entirely?"

She snapped a series of photos with her phone, the flash illuminating the dusty attic in stark bursts of light. Each image captured another piece of the puzzle, another clue to unraveling the mystery of Mark's disappearance.

As she reached the final page, Reyes froze, her breath catching in her throat. There, in the center of the page, was a drawing of a device she'd never seen before. A machine that looked like it could tear apart the very fabric of reality.

"What the fuck did you build, Mark?" she whispered, a sense of dread settling in the pit of her stomach. "And where the hell are you now?"

Reyes snapped one final photo and closed the journal with a decisive thud. She knew she was on the verge of something huge, something that could crack this case wide open. But she also knew that the deeper she dug, the more dangerous things would become.

"Screw it," she muttered, tucking the journal under her arm. "I'm not backing down now. Not when I'm this close to the truth."

With a last glance around the attic, Reyes descended the stairs, her mind whirling with questions and possibilities. She had a lead, a real lead, and she'd be damned if she let it slip through her fingers.

Reyes burst out of the Jennings' house, her heart pounding with a mixture of excitement and trepidation. The leather-bound journal felt heavy in her hands, weighted with the secrets it contained. She strode towards her car, her mind already racing ahead to the next steps in her investigation.

As she reached for the door handle, a sudden movement in her peripheral vision made her freeze. Her hand instinctively reached for her gun, but she relaxed slightly when she realized it was just Rachel, standing on the front porch with her arms wrapped tightly around herself.

"Did you find something?" Rachel called out, her voice trembling with a mixture of hope and fear.

Reyes hesitated, weighing her words carefully. "I found a lead," she said finally, her tone measured. "But I need to do some more digging before I can say anything for sure."

Rachel nodded, her eyes glistening with unshed tears. "Just... just bring him home, Detective. Please."

Reyes felt a pang of sympathy for the woman, but she pushed it aside. She couldn't afford to get emotional, not now. Not when she was so close to the truth.

"I'll do everything in my power to find him," she said, her voice firm with conviction. "I promise you that."

With a final nod, Reyes slid into her car and gunned the engine. As she pulled away from the curb, she glanced in the rearview mirror, watching as Rachel's figure grew smaller and smaller until it disappeared entirely.

"Alright, Mark," she muttered under her breath, her eyes narrowing with determination. "It's time to figure out what the hell you've gotten yourself into."

She reached for her phone, scrolling through her contacts until she found the name she was looking for. Dr. Ethan Novak, a brilliant physicist who'd helped her on a case a few years back. If anyone could make sense of the strange symbols and diagrams in Mark's journal, it was him.

As the phone rang, Reyes tapped her fingers impatiently against the steering wheel. She had a feeling that this case was about to take a turn for the bizarre, but she was ready for it. Ready to follow the trail wherever it led, no matter how dark or dangerous it might become.

Because that's who she was. Detective Samantha Reyes, the one who never backed down from a challenge. The one who always got her man, no matter the cost.

And this time, she had a feeling that the cost would be higher than ever before.

The apartment was a goddamn disaster, just like her life. Samantha Reyes sat amidst the chaos of scattered case files and newspaper clippings, all screaming the same name: Mark Jennings. She took a long drag from her cigarette, the smoke curling around her like a shroud. Her phone buzzed, the harsh sound cutting through the silence. An

THE HUSBAND

unknown number with a cryptic message: "Northern Canada. The truth awaits."

She stared at the screen, her thumb hovering over the delete button. Anonymous tips were a dime a dozen these days, each one more bat-shit crazy than the last. Tokyo, Buenos Aires, fucking Timbuktu - Jennings had apparently been busy racking up frequent flier miles.

"Ah, screw it," Reyes muttered, stubbing out her cigarette with more force than necessary. She had nothing left to lose. Her once-promising career had gone down in flames the moment she'd started chasing phantom sightings of Mark Jennings across the globe. The captain had made it crystal clear: drop the case or drop your badge.

She stood abruptly, sending papers flying.

The streetlights blurred together as Reyes sped through the city streets. Her knuckles whitened on the steering wheel as her mind raced with the strange accounts she'd gathered.

Mark Jennings spotted in a Tokyo karaoke bar. The same night, seen stumbling out of a Buenos Aires nightclub. How the hell was this guy pulling off this Houdini act?

She shook her head, trying to make sense of it all. The impossibility of it gnawed at her, but she couldn't let it go. Not when she was this close.

Reyes pulled up to the small airstrip, tires screeching on the asphalt. In the dim light, she could make out the silhouette of a small plane and a figure leaning against it, cigarette in hand.

She stepped out, slamming the car door behind her. The figure turned, revealing a grizzled face partially obscured by an aviator cap.

"You Reyes?" he grunted.

She nodded curtly. "You got a name?"

"Don't need one for this. Cash only. We'll be flying low, under the radar."

Reyes pulled out a wad of bills from her coat pocket, the last of her savings. She tossed it to the pilot.

"Just get me there in one piece."

The pilot smirked, pocketing the cash. "No promises in this rust bucket. But I'll do my best."

He stubbed out his cigarette and climbed into the cockpit. Reyes took a deep breath and followed, the small plane creaking under her weight.

This is it, she thought as the propeller sputtered to life. *Answers or bust. And I'll be damned if I don't get to the bottom of this.*

The plane lurched forward, picking up speed down the runway. Reyes gripped the armrests, her stomach dropping as they lifted off into the night sky, heading towards the frozen north and the strangeness that awaited her.

The turbulence jostled Reyes in her seat as she squinted at her phone, trying to make out the details of the anonymous tip through the scratched screen. It mentioned a gathering of Mark Jennings look-alikes in some godforsaken corner of the Canadian wilderness, all speaking in an unknown tongue.

"How much longer?" she shouted over the din of the propeller.

The pilot glanced back, his weathered face impassive. "Fifteen, maybe twenty." His voice was a gruff rasp, barely audible.

Reyes grunted in acknowledgment, stuffing the phone back in her pocket. The stained fabric of the seat chafed against her jeans. She rubbed her eyes, weary from another sleepless night spent poring over files.

The plane lurched as it hit a patch of rough air. Reyes gripped the armrests, her knuckles whitening. She had never been a fan of flying, even less so in a rust bucket like this. But it was the only way to reach the coordinates from the tip.

Her mind churned with possibilities. Multiple Mark Jennings sightings, stretched across the globe. A gathering in the middle of nowhere. An unknown language. None of it made a lick of sense. But if there was even a chance of getting some answers, of proving she wasn't just some crackpot with a hard-on for the bizarre, she had to take it.

The plane dipped, angling for a landing. Reyes leaned forward, peering out the scratched window. An improvised runway stretched through a gap in the thick carpet of pines, little more than a dirt track dusted with snow.

The wheels hit the ground with a jarring thud. Reyes braced herself against the seat in front of her as the plane bounced and skidded before finally shuddering to a stop.

She pulled her coat tighter around herself and grabbed her duffel bag from under the seat. The pilot was already unlatching the door, letting in a blast of frigid air that stole the breath from her lungs.

Reyes hopped down onto the packed snow, sinking to her ankles. She scanned the tree line, her hand resting on the butt of her gun. Nothing but an endless sea of green and white.

"I'll be back in three hours," the pilot said, already climbing back into the cockpit. "If you're not here, I'm gone. I don't get paid enough for this shit."

"Noted." Reyes shouldered her bag, the snow crunching under her boots as she started her trek into the woods. The cold air burned her throat with each breath. Every fiber of her being screamed that this was insanity. Chasing ghosts and shadows into the frozen ass-crack of the world.

But she was done playing by the rules. Done being the butt of every joke at the precinct. This was her chance to prove them all wrong.

And she'd walk through hell itself to do it.

The forest closed in around her, the towering pines blocking out the weak northern sun. Reyes' breath puffed out in white clouds as she navigated the uneven terrain, her mind wandering back to the snide comments and snickers that had followed her for months.

"Doppelgängers? Really, Samantha?" Detective Lopez had scoffed, leaning back in his chair with a smirk. "What's next, evil twins from an alternate dimension?"

"I'm telling you, there's more to this case than meets the eye," Reyes had insisted, but her words fell on deaf ears. They'd written her off as a crackpot, a once-promising detective losing her grip on reality.

She gritted her teeth, pushing the memories aside. They'd see. When she dragged the truth back from this godforsaken wilderness, they'd all see.

A twig snapped somewhere off to her left, and Reyes froze, her hand flying to her holster. She scanned the trees, heart pounding in her ears. Another snap, closer this time. She drew her gun, the cold metal biting into her palm.

Then, through the trees, she spotted it. A clearing up ahead, three figures standing in a circle. Reyes dropped into a crouch, creeping forward until she was hidden behind a massive oak. Her breath caught in her throat as she peered around the trunk.

It was them. The Jennings doppelgängers. They stood with their backs to her, their heads bowed together as if in deep conversation. Reyes' hand shook as she raised her phone, zooming in to capture their faces.

"Come on, you bastards," she muttered under her breath. "What the hell are you up to out here?"

Her finger hovered over the record button, ready to capture the evidence that would vindicate her once and for all. She leaned forward, straining to catch a snippet of their conversation.

But then, as if sensing her presence, one of the figures turned, his eyes locking onto hers across the clearing. Reyes' blood ran cold.

They'd seen her. And from the looks on their faces, they weren't happy about it.

In a heartbeat, the three doppelgängers whirled to face her, their voices rising in a discordant symphony of anger. The language they spoke was unlike anything Reyes had ever heard, a guttural mix of harsh consonants and serpentine vowels that sent shivers down her spine.

"Shit," Reyes hissed, fumbling with her phone as she tried to capture the scene unfolding before her. Her fingers, numb from the biting cold, slipped on the smooth screen, nearly dropping the device into the snow.

She managed to hit record, the red light blinking to life just as the Jennings copies began to advance on her position. Their movements were fluid, almost unnaturally graceful, as they closed the distance between them with alarming speed.

Reyes' heart hammered against her ribs, adrenaline surging through her veins as she weighed her options. She could stand her ground, confront these... things head-on and demand answers. Or she could run, disappear into the forest and hope to God they didn't catch her.

But she'd come too far to back down now. Too many sleepless nights, too many whispered rumors and sideways glances from her colleagues. She needed this, needed to prove that she wasn't just some crackpot with a wild theory.

Steeling herself, Reyes stepped out from behind the tree, her gun raised and her phone held aloft. The doppelgängers halted their approach, their expressions unreadable as they regarded her with those eerily familiar eyes.

"All right, you sons of bitches," Reyes called out, her voice steady despite the fear churning in her gut. "Time to start talking. What the hell are you, and what do you want with Mark Jennings?"

The Marks remained silent, their gazes locked on Reyes as they stood in a loose semi-circle around her. The cold wind whistled through the trees, carrying with it the scent of pine and something else, something alien and unsettling.

Reyes tightened her grip on her gun, the metal warm against her palm. "I'm not fucking around here," she growled, her breath fogging in the frigid air. "I've been chasing your asses for months, and I want answers. Now."

One of the Marks tilted his head, a strange, almost mechanical motion that sent a chill down Reyes' spine. When he spoke, his voice was a perfect imitation of Jennings', but there was an undercurrent of something else, a resonance that made her teeth ache.

"You have no idea what you're dealing with, Detective Reyes," he said, his lips curling into a smirk. "You're in over your head, and you know it."

Reyes barked a laugh, the sound harsh and humorless. "Story of my fucking life," she retorted, her eyes darting between the three figures. "But I'm not leaving here without the truth. So start talking, or I start shooting."

The Marks exchanged glances, a silent communication that set Reyes' nerves on edge. She could feel the weight of their scrutiny, the unnatural stillness of their bodies as they regarded her with a mixture of curiosity and disdain.

"The truth?" another Mark asked, his voice a perfect echo of the first. "You couldn't handle the truth, Detective. It would shatter your fragile human mind, leave you a gibbering wreck."

Reyes' finger tightened on the trigger, her heart pounding in her ears. She knew she was outmatched, knew that these things could probably kill her without breaking a sweat. But she'd be damned if she'd let them see her fear.

"Try me," she said, her voice low and dangerous. "I've seen some shit in my time, and I'm still standing. So start talking, or I start putting holes in you. Your choice."

The Marks' eyes glowed with an otherworldly light, their faces splitting into identical, predatory grins. Reyes felt a surge of terror, a primal instinct screaming at her to run, to get as far away from these things as possible.

But she stood her ground, her gun steady and her resolve unshakeable. Whatever happened next, she was ready for it. She had to be.

Without warning, the three Marks began to glow, a strange light emanating from their bodies. The air around them shimmered and pulsed, like the heat rising from a scorching desert. Reyes watched in disbelief as their skin crackled and split, revealing a pulsating network of luminescent veins beneath.

"What the fuck?" she breathed, her gun wavering as she struggled to comprehend the sight before her.

The Marks spoke in unison, their voices reverberating with an otherworldly echo. "You have no idea what you've stumbled into, Detective. Forces beyond your comprehension, a war that has raged across the cosmos for eons."

Reyes' mind reeled, trying to process their words. "What are you talking about? What war? What the hell are you?"

The Marks merely smiled, their faces now fully ablaze with the eerie light. "We are the harbingers of a new age, the vanguard of a revolution that will reshape the very fabric of reality."

As they spoke, their bodies began to combust, flames licking at their clothes and hair. Reyes staggered back, shielding her face from the intense heat. She watched in horror as the Marks disintegrated before her eyes, their flesh and bone crumbling to ash in a matter of seconds.

And then, as abruptly as it had begun, it was over. The clearing fell silent, the only sound the ragged gasps of Reyes' breath. She lowered her gun, her hands shaking uncontrollably.

"Jesus Christ," she muttered, running a trembling hand through her hair. "What the actual fuck just happened?"

Stunned, Reyes approached the spot where the Marks had stood, her mind racing to comprehend what she had just witnessed. The snow around the area had melted, leaving a patch of scorched earth and smoldering ashes.

She knelt down, sifting through the remains with the barrel of her gun. Amidst the ashes, a glint of something caught her eye. She reached out, her fingers closing around a charred pamphlet.

Brushing away the soot, Reyes examined the cover. It was covered in strange hieroglyphs, symbols unlike anything she had ever seen before. They seemed to writhe and shift before her eyes, as if alive.

"What the hell is this?" she whispered, her brow furrowed in confusion and trepidation.

She tucked the pamphlet into her coat pocket, her mind already racing with the implications of her discovery. Whatever this was, whatever those things had been, it was bigger than anything she had ever encountered before.

Reyes stood up, brushing the ash from her knees. She took one last look around the clearing, at the spot where the Marks had burned away to nothing. Then, with a deep breath and a newfound sense of purpose, she turned and began the long trek back to her waiting plane.

As the rickety plane carried her back to civilization, Reyes couldn't shake the feeling that she had stumbled onto something far bigger than she had ever imagined. The charred pamphlet felt heavy in her pocket, a tangible reminder of the impossible things she had witnessed.

She pulled it out, running her fingers over the strange hieroglyphs once more. "What the fuck are you trying to tell me?" she muttered, as if the symbols could answer her questions.

Reyes knew she couldn't go back to her old life, not after what she had seen. The Marks, their bizarre language, the way they had burned away to nothing - it all pointed to something beyond human understanding.

She leaned back in her seat, closing her eyes as the plane's engines droned on. In her mind's eye, she could see the Marks standing in that clearing, their faces identical to the man she had been chasing for so long.

"Mark Jennings, what the hell are you mixed up in?" she whispered, her breath fogging the plane's window.

Reyes knew she had to find answers, no matter the cost. She had come too far, sacrificed too much, to turn back now. The truth was out there, waiting to be uncovered, and she was determined to be the one to bring it to light.

As the plane touched down on the airstrip, Reyes felt a renewed sense of purpose coursing through her veins. She had a lead, a clue that could finally help her unravel the mystery of Mark Jennings and his impossible doppelgängers.

She stepped out of the plane, the pamphlet tucked safely in her pocket, and strode towards her car with a grim smile on her face. The game was on, and Samantha Reyes was ready to play.

Detective Samantha Reyes trudged through the dense, snow-laden forest of northern Canada, her breath visible in the frigid air. She clutched her Glock 22 tightly, her eyes scanning the desolate landscape for any sign of movement. The crunch of her boots against the frozen ground was the only sound that pierced the eerie stillness.

"Fucking freezing out here," Reyes muttered under her breath, her chapped lips stinging from the cold. She'd been on this wild goose chase for hours, following a lead that seemed more like a dead end with each passing minute. But she was too stubborn to give up now.

A faint, unfamiliar sound carried by the wind caught her attention, drawing her gaze to a clearing up ahead. Reyes narrowed her eyes, trying to make out the source of the noise. Her instincts kicked into high gear, urging her to approach with caution.

She crept forward, her heart pounding with a mix of fear and determination. The hairs on the back of her neck stood on end as she inched closer to the clearing. Reyes tightened her grip on the Glock, ready to face whatever lay ahead.

"Better not be another fucking false alarm," she growled, her breath forming icy clouds in front of her face. The sound grew louder as she neared the edge of the clearing. It was an odd, guttural noise, unlike anything she'd heard before.

Reyes paused at the tree line, her pulse racing. She took a deep breath, steeling herself for whatever awaited her. With a final surge of resolve, she stepped out from the cover of the forest and into the unknown.

As she stepped into the clearing, Reyes froze, her eyes widening in disbelief. There, standing in a tense triangle, were three identical versions of Mark Jennings. Their voices were raised in a heated argument, the alien language they spoke sharp and guttural, echoing eerily in the stillness.

"What the actual fuck?" Reyes muttered under her breath, her mind racing to make sense of the impossible sight before her. She blinked hard, half-expecting the Marks to vanish like some sort of surreal mirage. But they remained, their faces contorted with anger as they continued their incomprehensible dispute.

Reyes felt a wave of vertigo wash over her, the ground seeming to tilt beneath her feet. She steadied herself, drawing in a sharp breath of icy air. This was beyond anything she'd encountered in her years on the force. Hell, it was beyond anything she'd ever imagined possible.

"Get your shit together, Reyes," she whispered harshly, forcing herself to focus. She couldn't afford to lose her cool, not now. Whatever this bizarre situation was, she had to confront it head-on.

The Marks continued to argue, their voices rising and falling in an unsettling rhythm. They seemed oblivious to her presence, lost in their own otherworldly conflict. Reyes studied them intently, trying to spot any differences between the three figures. But they were identical in every way, from their clothing to their mannerisms.

"This is some next-level Twilight Zone bullshit," Reyes muttered, shaking her head in disbelief. She'd seen her fair share of strange cases, but this was a whole new level of weird.

Taking a deep breath, Reyes straightened her shoulders and tightened her grip on the Glock. She knew she had to act, to take control of the situation before it spiraled any further into insanity. With a determined stride, she stepped forward, ready to confront the impossible head-on.

"Hey, assholes!" she called out, her voice cutting through the eerie stillness of the clearing. "Time to start making some fucking sense."

The Marks froze, their argument abruptly silenced by Reyes' sharp command. In unnerving synchronicity, they turned to face her, their movements mirrored with unsettling precision. Reyes felt a chill run down her spine as six identical eyes locked onto her, their gazes intense and unreadable.

"Detective Reyes," the Marks spoke in unison, their voices blending into a single, haunting tone. "We've been expecting you."

Reyes fought the urge to take a step back, refusing to show any sign of weakness. "Cut the creepy hive-mind bullshit," she snapped, her finger resting on the trigger of her Glock. "I want answers, and I want them now."

The Marks tilted their heads to the side, a gesture that would have been comical if not for the unnatural coordination. "Answers are subjective, Detective," they replied, their lips curling into identical, unsettling smiles. "The truth you seek may not be the truth you desire."

Reyes gritted her teeth, frustration mingling with the growing sense of unease in her gut. She'd dealt with her share of cryptic assholes before, but this was taking it to a whole new level. "I'm not here to play fucking riddles," she growled, taking a menacing step forward. "Start talking, or I start shooting."

The Marks remained unfazed, their eyes glinting with an otherworldly amusement. "Violence will not serve you here, Detective," they chided, their voices laced with a condescending edge. "The path to understanding lies beyond the realm of physical force."

Reyes fought the urge to put a bullet between their smug, identical eyes. This was getting her nowhere fast. She needed a new approach, a way to throw them off balance and gain the upper hand. Her mind raced, searching for a crack in their eerie façade.

"Alright, you trippy bastards," she said, lowering her weapon slightly. "You want to play games? Let's play. But I'm warning you, I don't lose."

The Marks' smiles widened, a glimmer of something dark and ancient flashing in their eyes. "The game has already begun, Detective," they intoned, their voices echoing with an ominous weight. "And the rules are not of your making."

Reyes felt a chill run down her spine, the weight of their words settling like a cold shadow in her chest. She'd faced down murderers and madmen, but this? This was something else entirely. The Marks stood before her, identical in every way, their very existence defying the laws of reality as she knew it.

"Enough with the cryptic bullshit," she snapped, her grip tightening on her weapon. "I want answers, and I want them now. Who the fuck are you, and what the hell is going on here?"

The Marks tilted their heads in unison, a gesture that sent a fresh wave of unease rippling through Reyes. "We are the harbingers of a truth that lies beyond your comprehension," they replied, their voices blending into a single, haunting melody. "A truth that will shatter the very foundations of your world."

Reyes scoffed, her jaw clenching with a mixture of anger and frustration. "I've heard that line before, usually from the mouths of delusional cultists and self-proclaimed prophets. What makes you any different?"

The Marks' eyes flashed with an otherworldly light, their expressions shifting from amusement to something darker, more primal. "We are not mere mortals, bound by the limitations of flesh and bone," they intoned, their voices thrumming with an ancient power.

"We are the embodiment of a force that transcends time and space, a force that will reshape the very fabric of existence."

Reyes felt her heart pounding in her chest, a cold sweat breaking out across her brow. Every instinct screamed at her to run, to flee this place and never look back. But she was a cop, dammit, and cops don't run from the truth, no matter how ugly or terrifying it might be.

She steadied her breath, her eyes narrowing with a fierce determination. "Alright, you interdimensional freakshows," she growled, her voice low and dangerous. "You want to play games? Let's dance. But I'm warning you, I play for keeps."

The Marks' smiles widened, a flicker of something ancient and terrible dancing in their eyes. "As do we, Detective," they whispered, their voices echoing with a sinister promise. "As do we."

The air in the clearing turned frigid, the temperature plummeting with each passing second. Reyes watched, transfixed, as the Marks began to move in unison, their bodies swaying to an unheard rhythm. Their eyes glowed brighter, the otherworldly light casting eerie shadows across their identical features.

Reyes tightened her grip on her weapon, her finger hovering over the trigger. She knew, deep down, that bullets would be useless against whatever the hell these things were, but the familiar weight of the gun in her hand brought a small measure of comfort.

The Marks spoke as one, their voices blending into a haunting chorus. "You cannot stop what is to come, Detective. The wheels of fate have already been set in motion, and the time of reckoning draws near."

"Spare me the cryptic bullshit," Reyes spat, her eyes flashing with defiance. "You want to talk about fate? I make my own damn fate."

The Marks laughed, the sound harsh and grating, like nails on a chalkboard. "Such bravado, such foolish pride. You are but a speck in the grand tapestry of the universe, a fleeting moment in the endless march of time."

Reyes felt a chill run down her spine, a primal fear clawing at the edges of her mind. She shook it off, refusing to let these bastards get under her skin. "You know what? Fuck you and your grand tapestry. I'm not here for a philosophy lesson. I'm here for answers."

The wind picked up, howling through the trees like a wounded animal. The Marks' eyes flashed with a malevolent glee, their voices rising above the gale. "Answers you shall have, Detective. But be warned, the truth you seek may be more than your mortal mind can bear."

Reyes gritted her teeth, her heart hammering in her chest. She knew she was in over her head, that she was facing something far beyond her understanding. But she'd be damned if she let these smug assholes see her sweat. "Try me," she growled, her voice dripping with venom. "I've faced worse than you on a slow Tuesday."

As the Marks began to glow more intensely, Reyes felt the ground vibrate beneath her feet. The air became charged with an electric energy, making the hairs on her arms stand on end. She watched in a mix of awe and terror as their forms grew brighter, the otherworldly light casting eerie shadows across the snow-covered clearing.

"What the hell?" Reyes muttered under her breath, her grip tightening on her weapon. She'd seen some weird shit in her time on the force, but this was a whole new level of fucked up.

The Marks' voices echoed in her mind, their words reverberating with a power that sent shivers down her spine. "You stand on the precipice of a great revelation, Detective. A truth that will shatter the very foundations of your reality."

Reyes took a step back, her instincts screaming at her to retreat, to get as far away from this insanity as possible. But her resolve kept her rooted in place, a stubborn determination to see this through, no matter the cost. "I'm not going anywhere until I get some straight answers," she barked, her voice cutting through the eerie hum of energy.

THE HUSBAND

The Marks' laughter filled the air, a sound that seemed to come from everywhere and nowhere at once. "Straight answers are a luxury you can ill afford, Detective. The path before you is twisted and treacherous, a labyrinth of secrets and lies."

Reyes felt a surge of anger, a burning desire to wipe the smug looks off their identical faces. "Enough with the cryptic bullshit," she snarled, her finger hovering over the trigger. "Start talking, or I start shooting."

The Marks' eyes flashed with amusement, their glowing forms pulsing with an intensity that made Reyes' head throb. "

The energy around the Marks reached a fever pitch, their bodies pulsing with an otherworldly radiance. Reyes narrowed her eyes against the blinding light as they merged into one, like some kind of fucked-up magic trick. Their forms grew indistinct, swallowed by the white hot glow.

"What the hell is happening?" Reyes muttered under her breath, her heart hammering against her ribs. She took an involuntary step back, shielding her face with her forearm. Every cell in her body screamed at her to run, but morbid fascination kept her rooted to the spot.

The light intensified to an unbearable level, the Marks now just a shapeless silhouette at its center. Reyes' mind reeled, trying and failing to make sense of the impossible spectacle. "This can't be real," she thought, jaw clenched. "I'm losing my goddamn mind out here."

Without warning, the light exploded outward in a sudden burst, engulfing the entire clearing. Reyes staggered back, momentarily blinded. "Shit!" she hissed, blinking furiously to clear the spots from her vision. Disoriented, she swept her gaze across the now empty clearing, her breath coming in ragged gasps.

The Marks had vanished without a trace, as if they'd never existed at all. "Where the fuck did they go?" Reyes growled, turning in a slow circle, weapon at the ready. But she was alone, with only the howling wind and pristine snow for company. "Son of a bitch," she spat, a chill that had nothing to do with the cold seeping into her bones.

As the adrenaline ebbed, a profound sense of unease settled over Reyes. She lowered her weapon, scanning the ground for any sign of the Marks' presence. That's when she spotted it - a charred pamphlet half-buried in the snow at her feet. "What the hell?" she muttered, crouching down to get a closer look.

With a gloved hand, Reyes brushed away the snow and gingerly picked up the pamphlet. The edges were singed, the paper brittle and blackened. But what caught her attention were the strange hieroglyphs that covered the front page - alien symbols that seemed to writhe and shift before her eyes. "Jesus Christ," she breathed, a shiver running down her spine. "What is this thing?"

Reyes' mind raced with questions, each more unsettling than the last. The Marks, the blinding light, and now this cryptic pamphlet - it all pointed to something far beyond her understanding. She shook her head, trying to clear the fog of confusion. "I need to get this back to the lab," she muttered, carefully tucking the pamphlet into her jacket pocket. "Maybe they can make some goddamn sense of it."

With one last glance at the empty clearing, Reyes turned and trudged back into the forest, her boots crunching through the snow. The weight of the pamphlet felt like a lead weight against her chest, a tangible reminder of the impossible events she'd just witnessed. "This is gonna be one hell of a report," she thought wryly, a humorless chuckle escaping her lips. "They'll probably think I've lost my fucking mind."

But Reyes knew what she'd seen, and she was determined to unravel the mystery, no matter where it led her. As the trees closed in around her, she set her jaw and quickened her pace, the alien hieroglyphs burned into her memory like a brand. The game was on, and Samantha Reyes was ready to play.

The three Marks stood in a tense standoff, their voices rising in a cacophony of guttural consonants and sing-song vowels that echoed through the remote Canadian wilderness. Their words were alien, incomprehensible, yet the urgency and fury in their tones needed no translation.

Detective Samantha Reyes approached cautiously, her Glock 22 drawn and aimed steadily at the identical figures. Her eyes darted between them, trying to identify any discernible difference, any hint of which one was the real Mark Finley. But they were perfect replicas, down to the small scar above the left eyebrow.

"What the fuck is going on here?" Reyes muttered under her breath. Her heart pounded against her ribcage like a caged animal desperate for escape. Fear tangled with determination in her gut as she inched closer, the gravel crunching beneath her boots.

The Marks continued arguing, oblivious to her presence. Their voices grew louder, more frantic, their words tripping over each other in a verbal melee. Reyes tightened her grip on the gun, a bead of sweat rolling down her temple. She had to get control of the situation, and fast.

"Hey! Shut the hell up and put your hands where I can see them!" Her shout cut through the argumental din like a knife.

The Marks froze, their gazes snapping to her in unison. Six identical eyes, cold and calculating, bore into her with an intensity that made Reyes' skin crawl. A heartbeat of silence passed, the tension thick enough to choke on.

Then, all hell broke loose.

Without warning, the air around the Marks shimmered, like a mirage in the desert heat. Reyes blinked, thinking it was a trick of the light, but the shimmering intensified, enveloping the identical figures in an ethereal glow.

"What the—"

Before she could finish her sentence, the Marks burst into flames simultaneously. The blinding light seared Reyes' retinas, forcing her to shield her eyes with her free hand. The intense heat rolled over her in waves, stealing the breath from her lungs.

"Jesus Christ!" Reyes stumbled back, her mind reeling as she tried to process the surreal sight before her.

The roar of the fire filled her ears, drowning out the startled curses that fell from her lips. The flames consumed the Marks in an instant, their bodies engulfed in a wild inferno. It was like something out of a nightmare, a twisted version of spontaneous human combustion.

Reyes' heart raced, slamming against her ribs with each frantic beat. She couldn't tear her eyes away from the horrific scene, even as the brightness burned into her vision. Disbelief warred with the undeniable reality unfolding in front of her.

"This can't be happening," she whispered, her voice barely audible over the crackling of the flames. "It's not possible."

But the heat on her face and the acrid smell of burning flesh told her otherwise. Reyes fought the urge to retch, her stomach churning as she watched the Marks disintegrate before her eyes.

Questions raced through her mind at breakneck speed. What had caused this? Some sort of chemical reaction? A hidden weapon? Or something far more sinister and unexplainable?

Reyes forced herself to breathe, to focus on the present moment, even as her world tilted on its axis. She had to keep it together, to find answers amidst the chaos. But as the flames danced and swirled, casting eerie shadows across the charred ground, she couldn't shake the feeling that she was in over her head.

As the blinding light faded, Reyes blinked rapidly, desperate to clear the searing afterimages from her vision. She coughed and sputtered, waving away the thick, acrid smoke that filled the air, stinging her eyes and burning her lungs.

"Fuck me sideways," she muttered, her voice raspy from the harsh fumes. "What the hell just happened?"

THE HUSBAND

Reyes staggered forward, her boots crunching on the charred ground as she approached the spot where the Marks had stood just moments before. The earth was scorched, a blackened circle that stood out in stark contrast against the lush green of the surrounding forest.

Her mind raced with a thousand questions, each more unsettling than the last. The Marks had been arguing, their voices rising in that strange, guttural language, and then... nothing. Just a burst of light and heat that had consumed them whole.

Reyes shook her head, trying to clear the cobwebs. She couldn't afford to lose focus, not now. There had to be an explanation, some clue that would make sense of this madness.

She scanned the area, her eyes darting from the smoldering ground to the trees beyond, searching for anything out of place. But the forest remained still and silent, as if mocking her with its tranquility.

"Think, Reyes, think," she muttered, running a hand through her sweat-dampened hair. "There's got to be something here, some piece of the puzzle."

But as she stood there, surrounded by the remnants of the impossible, Reyes couldn't shake the feeling that she was in over her head. Whatever had happened here, it was far beyond anything she'd ever encountered before.

She took a deep breath, the acrid taste of smoke still lingering on her tongue. There was no turning back now. She had to see this through, no matter where it led her.

With a newfound resolve, Reyes squared her shoulders and began to methodically search the area, her eyes peeled for any clue that might shed light on the bizarre events that had just unfolded. The truth was out there, and she'd be damned if she didn't find it.

As Reyes combed through the charred remains, her boots kicking up clouds of ash with each step, something caught her eye. Amidst the blackened debris, a glint of color stood out like a beacon.

"What the hell?" she muttered, crouching down for a closer look.

It was a pamphlet, its edges curled and singed, but somehow still intact. Reyes reached out tentatively, her fingers hovering just above the strange artifact.

"This doesn't make any goddamn sense," she said, shaking her head. "How did this survive the fire?"

Curiosity getting the better of her, Reyes gingerly picked up the pamphlet, brushing away the clinging ash. As she examined it more closely, her eyes widened in disbelief.

The pamphlet was covered in bizarre symbols, unlike anything she'd ever seen before. They seemed to shift and morph before her eyes, dancing across the page in a mesmerizing pattern.

"Holy shit," Reyes breathed, her heart pounding in her chest. "What is this?"

She ran her fingers over the strange hieroglyphs, tracing their alien contours. The symbols felt warm to the touch, almost alive, as if they were pulsing with some unknowable energy.

Reyes knew she should be cautious, that touching the pamphlet could be dangerous. But the pull of the unknown was too strong to resist. She had to know what it meant, what secrets it held.

With a deep breath, Reyes flipped open the pamphlet, her eyes scanning the pages hungrily. The symbols seemed to leap out at her, their meaning just beyond her grasp.

"Come on, Reyes, you've cracked tougher codes than this," she muttered, her brow furrowed in concentration.

But as she delved deeper into the pamphlet's mysteries, Reyes couldn't shake the feeling that she was treading on forbidden ground. The symbols seemed to whisper to her, promising knowledge beyond her wildest dreams, but at what cost?

She shook her head, trying to clear the strange thoughts from her mind. She was a detective, dammit, not some wide-eyed mystic. She had to stay grounded, focus on the facts.

But as Reyes looked up from the pamphlet, she realized that the world around her had changed. The forest seemed to shimmer and warp, as if reality itself was bending to the will of the alien symbols.

"What the fuck?" she whispered, her voice barely audible over the pounding of her heart.

She knew she should put the pamphlet down, walk away before it was too late. But the pull of the unknown was too strong. Reyes had to see this through, no matter where it led her.

With a deep breath, she tucked the pamphlet into her jacket pocket and stood up, her eyes scanning the horizon. Whatever lay ahead, she was ready to face it head-on.

The disorientation hit her like a freight train, sending her staggering back a step. The world tilted on its axis, colors bleeding together in a dizzying kaleidoscope. Reyes blinked hard, trying to regain her bearings, but the vertigo only intensified.

"Shit, shit, shit," she hissed through clenched teeth, her fingers digging into her palms as she fought to stay upright.

It was as if the very fabric of reality was unraveling around her, the threads of existence coming undone one by one. The air felt thick and heavy, pressing down on her like a physical weight.

Reyes forced herself to take a deep breath, focusing on the sensation of the cool air filling her lungs. Slowly, the world began to right itself, the colors settling back into their proper places.

But even as the disorientation faded, Reyes couldn't shake the eerie feeling that something had fundamentally changed. The forest around her seemed different somehow, the shadows deeper and more menacing.

She glanced down at the pamphlet in her hand, the alien symbols seeming to mock her with their indecipherable meanings. What the hell had she gotten herself into?

Reyes shook her head, a humorless laugh escaping her lips. "You've really done it this time, haven't you?" she muttered to herself.

But even as the words left her mouth, Reyes knew there was no turning back now. The pamphlet held the key to unlocking this mystery, and she'd be damned if she let a little existential crisis stop her from seeing it through.

With a newfound sense of determination, Reyes squared her shoulders and scanned the clearing, half-expecting the Marks to materialize out of thin air. But the only sound was the rustling of the wind through the trees, the only movement the swaying of the branches.

"Alright, you bastards," she said, her voice low and fierce. "You want to play games? Let's fucking play."

Reyes tucked the pamphlet securely into her pocket, her hand brushing against the cool metal of her gun. Whatever lay ahead, she was ready to face it head-on. The truth was out there, and she'd stop at nothing to find it.

Reyes strode purposefully through the forest, her boots crunching against the charred ground. The weight of the pamphlet in her pocket seemed to grow with each step, a tangible reminder of the impossible events she'd witnessed.

Her mind raced, trying to make sense of it all. The Marks, their strange argument, the sudden burst of flames - it defied all logic, all reason. And yet, the evidence was right there, tucked securely against her hip.

"Get it together, Reyes," she muttered, shaking her head. "You've seen some weird shit before, but this takes the fucking cake."

She thought back to her training, the countless hours spent honing her skills as a detective. But nothing could have prepared her for this. It was like something out of a goddamn science fiction novel, and she was the unwitting protagonist thrust into the middle of it all.

As she walked, Reyes found herself questioning everything she thought she knew. The world seemed to shift and warp around her, the once-familiar forest now alien and unsettling. She half-expected to see the Marks materialize from behind a tree, their voices echoing in that strange language once more.

But the only sound was the pounding of her own heart, the ragged breath escaping her lungs. Reyes clenched her jaw, determination coursing through her veins. She wouldn't let this break her, wouldn't let the fear and uncertainty take hold.

"You've got this, Reyes," she said, her voice barely above a whisper. "You've faced worse before, and you'll face worse again. This is just another case, another mystery to solve."

She reached into her pocket, her fingers brushing against the pamphlet once more. It was a lifeline, a promise of answers to come. And Reyes would stop at nothing to uncover the truth, no matter how strange or terrifying it might be.

With renewed resolve, she quickened her pace, the forest blurring around her. The road ahead was uncertain, but Reyes was ready to face whatever lay in store. She had a job to do, and she'd be damned if she let anything stand in her way.

Reyes' mind raced as she trekked through the forest, the eerie stillness broken only by the crunch of her boots against the ground. The impossible events she'd witnessed played on repeat, a twisted highlight reel she couldn't shake.

"Spontaneous human combustion? Alien hieroglyphs? What the actual fuck?" she muttered, her brow furrowed in a mix of disbelief and frustration.

She'd seen her fair share of weird shit on the job, but this was a whole new level of bizarre. Reyes had always prided herself on her ability to compartmentalize, to keep a cool head in the face of the unknown. But now, with reality itself seeming to unravel, she found herself grasping for any semblance of normalcy.

The theories swirled in her mind, each more outlandish than the last. Government conspiracies, extraterrestrial involvement, ancient curses—none of it made sense, but what other explanation could there be?

"Get a grip, Reyes," she chided herself, shaking her head. "You're a detective, not a fucking sci-fi writer."

But even as she tried to rationalize, to find some logical thread to follow, the weight of the pamphlet in her pocket served as a constant reminder of the truth she couldn't ignore. The symbols seemed to burn against her skin, a silent promise of revelations to come.

Reyes quickened her pace, her eyes scanning the forest for any sign of her vehicle. She needed to get back to the station, to dive into the case files and start piecing together the clues. There had to be a connection, some thread that would unravel this mystery.

But as she walked, the forest seemed to shift and change around her, the shadows deepening and the silence growing heavier. Reyes felt a prickle of unease along her spine, a sense that she was being watched by unseen eyes.

"Just your imagination," she told herself, but her hand instinctively drifted towards her holster, the weight of her gun a reassuring presence.

The forest had always been a place of solace for Reyes, a sanctuary from the chaos of the city and the darkness of her job. But now, with the memory of the Marks' fiery demise seared into her mind, the once-familiar landscape felt alien and threatening.

She walked faster, her heart pounding in her chest as she wove between the trees. The pamphlet seemed to grow heavier with each step, a tangible reminder of the impossible truth she carried.

Reyes knew she was on the precipice of something big, something that would change everything she thought she knew about the world. And as much as the prospect terrified her, she couldn't deny the thrill of the chase, the rush of adrenaline that came with unraveling a mystery.

She was close now, the edge of the forest just ahead. Reyes could see the glint of metal through the trees, the familiar shape of her car a beacon of normalcy in the midst of the strange.

But even as she emerged from the forest, the weight of the unknown still pressed down on her, a constant companion in the journey ahead. Reyes knew there would be no turning back, no unseeing what she'd witnessed.

The truth was out there, waiting to be uncovered. And Detective Samantha Reyes was ready to face it head-on, no matter the cost.

Reyes reached her car, the sleek black sedan a welcome sight after the surreal events in the forest. She fished her keys from her pocket, her fingers trembling slightly as she unlocked the door and slid into the driver's seat.

The engine roared to life, and Reyes gripped the steering wheel, taking a moment to steady herself. She glanced at the pamphlet on the passenger seat, its alien hieroglyphs seeming to mock her, daring her to unravel their secrets.

"What the hell have I gotten myself into?" she muttered, shaking her head.

But even as the words left her lips, Reyes knew there was no going back. The Marks' death, the strange pamphlet, the energy crackling in the air—it all pointed to something bigger, something that demanded to be investigated.

She pulled out her phone, scrolling through her contacts until she found the one she needed. The call connected after two rings, and a gruff voice answered on the other end.

"Reyes? What's up?"

"Carson, I need you to run a trace on a pamphlet I found. It's got some kind of alien writing on it, like nothing I've ever seen before."

There was a pause, and then Carson's voice came back, tinged with skepticism. "Alien writing? You sure you're not just seeing things, Reyes?"

"Trust me, after what I just witnessed, I'm questioning everything," Reyes replied, her tone serious. "But this pamphlet, it's real. And I need to know what it means."

"All right, I'll see what I can dig up. But Reyes, be careful out there. If this is as big as you think it is, you might be stepping into something way over your head."

Reyes smiled grimly, her eyes fixed on the road ahead. "Story of my life, Carson. But I'm not backing down, not until I have answers."

She ended the call, tossing her phone onto the passenger seat beside the pamphlet. The road stretched out before her, a winding path into the unknown.

Reyes took a deep breath, her resolve hardening with each passing moment. She had a job to do, a mystery to solve, and nothing—not even the impossible—was going to stand in her way.

With a final glance at the pamphlet, Reyes put the car in drive and accelerated, ready to face whatever lay ahead in her quest for the truth.

Detective Vanessa Reyes burst through the precinct doors like a hurricane, dark eyes flashing with defiant fire as whispers and sidelong glances swirled around her. She strode past the worn desks and buzzing fluorescent lights, a woman on a mission with zero fucks left to give.

Let them gossip, she thought, jaw clenched. *I know what I saw.* The hellish scene in Canada still seared her mind—three identical versions of Mark Jennings, a language of unnerving hieroglyphs crackling through the air, flames erupting as logic shattered into a million pieces.

Reyes marched straight for the captain's office and rapped sharply on the door, not waiting for a response before barging in. Captain Briggs looked up from his cluttered desk, leaning back in his squeaky chair and crossing his arms. Skepticism was etched into the weathered lines of his face.

"Detective Reyes," he said gruffly. "I assume you have an explanation for this so-called report of yours?" He nodded at the file on his desk like it might bite him.

THE HUSBAND

Reyes met his gaze head-on. "Sir, I know how it sounds. But I'm telling you, it's all true. Every insane detail." Her voice was steady, but frustration simmered beneath the surface.

"Identical triplets speaking in tongues? Spontaneous combustion?" Briggs scoffed. "You expect me to believe that? You're supposed to be my best detective, Vanessa."

"Dammit, Captain!" She slammed a palm on his desk, the smack reverberating. "I was there. I know what I saw, and I know it doesn't make a lick of sense. But that doesn't change the facts."

Reyes began recounting the otherworldly events, each word precise and unrelenting. She described the eerie confrontation—a cacophony of guttural chants, the air shimmering with unnatural heat. The acrid stench of charred flesh. Three faces, all the same, mocking her with impossible truths...

As she laid out her findings, Reyes could feel the captain's doubt like a physical force pressing against her. But she would not yield. She'd walk through hellfire itself to uncover what really happened to Mark Jennings. For herself, and for his shattered wife Rachel.

There has to be an explanation, Reyes told herself fiercely. *And suspension be damned, I'm going to find it. This is only the beginning.*

The captain shook his head, a mix of disbelief and disappointment etched into his weathered features. "I'm sorry, Reyes, but I can't accept this. It's too far-fetched, even for you."

Reyes opened her mouth to protest, but he held up a hand, silencing her. "I have no choice but to suspend you, effective immediately. Turn in your badge and gun."

The words hit Reyes like a punch to the gut, knocking the wind out of her. She clenched her jaw, refusing to let the captain see her falter. With a curt nod, she unclipped her badge and placed it on his desk, followed by her service weapon. The cold metal seemed to burn her fingers as she let it go.

This can't be happening, Reyes thought, her mind reeling. *Not now, not when I'm so close to the truth.*

She turned on her heel and strode out of the office, her head held high despite the weight of her shattered career bearing down on her. The precinct buzzed with the usual chaos—ringing phones, shuffling papers, and the low hum of conversation—but Reyes felt like she was moving through molasses.

Each step felt heavy, as if her feet were encased in concrete. She could feel the eyes of her colleagues boring into her back, their whispers and sideways glances like daggers in her skin. Reyes pushed through the doors, desperate to escape the suffocating atmosphere.

The cold Connecticut air bit at her cheeks as she made her way to her car, a bitter reminder of the harsh reality she now faced. *Suspended. Powerless. Alone.* The words echoed in her mind, taunting her with their finality.

Reyes slid into the driver's seat, gripping the steering wheel until her knuckles turned white. She closed her eyes, taking a deep, shuddering breath. *No,* she thought fiercely. *I won't let this stop me. I'll find the truth, even if it means going rogue.*

With a newfound sense of determination, Reyes started the engine, the roar of the motor drowning out the doubts that threatened to consume her. She pulled out of the parking lot, ready to face whatever lay ahead, no matter the cost.

I'm coming for you, Mark Jennings, she vowed silently. *And heaven help anyone who stands in my way.*

Rachel Jennings sat on the couch, the framed photo of Mark clutched to her chest like a lifeline. The living room, once a haven of warmth and laughter, now felt cold and empty, a stark reflection of the void in her heart.

She stared at the smiling faces in the picture, their happiness forever frozen in time. *How could everything have gone so wrong?*

THE HUSBAND

Rachel wondered, her mind a whirlwind of confusion and betrayal. *What secrets were you hiding, Mark?*

The sound of a knock at the door startled her from her thoughts. Rachel set the photo down on the coffee table, wiping away the tears that had begun to fall unbidden. She stood, her legs shaky as she made her way to the door.

Through the peephole, she saw the familiar face of Detective Reyes, her expression a mix of determination and weariness. Rachel hesitated, her hand hovering over the doorknob. *Do I really want to hear what she has to say?*

Another knock, more insistent this time. Rachel took a deep breath, steeling herself for whatever lay ahead. She opened the door, revealing the detective standing on her doorstep, a gust of cold air swirling around them.

"Detective Reyes," Rachel said, her voice hoarse from crying. "What are you doing here?"

Reyes's eyes, bloodshot and tired, met Rachel's. "We need to talk, Mrs. Jennings. May I come in?"

Rachel stepped aside, allowing the detective to enter. As she closed the door behind them, she couldn't shake the feeling that her world was about to be turned upside down once again.

"I'm suspended," Reyes said bluntly, turning to face Rachel. "The captain didn't believe my report about what happened in Canada."

Rachel's eyes widened. "What? But why? What did you find?"

Reyes shook her head, a mirthless laugh escaping her lips. "You wouldn't believe me if I told you. Hell, I barely believe it myself."

"Try me," Rachel said, crossing her arms. "I think I deserve to know the truth, no matter how crazy it sounds."

The two women stood in the middle of Rachel's living room, the tension palpable. Reyes ran a hand through her disheveled hair, a sigh escaping her lips. She gestured to the couch, and they both sat down, the silence stretching between them like a chasm.

Reyes leaned forward, elbows resting on her knees. "I saw three Marks in Canada," she said, her voice low and urgent. "Three identical men, all claiming to be your husband."

Rachel's brow furrowed, disbelief etched into her features. "That's impossible. There's only one Mark, and he's missing."

"I know how it sounds," Reyes said, frustration seeping into her tone. "But I confronted them. They spoke in some strange language, like nothing I've ever heard before. And then..." She trailed off, her eyes distant.

"And then what?" Rachel demanded, her voice rising. "What happened?"

Reyes looked up, meeting Rachel's gaze. "They burst into flames," she said, the words hanging in the air like a death sentence. "All three of them, consumed by fire that came out of nowhere."

Rachel stood abruptly, her hands clenched into fists. "Is this some kind of sick joke?" she asked, her voice trembling with anger. "My husband is missing, and you're telling me you saw him burn to death in Canada?"

"I'm telling you the truth," Reyes said, her own frustration bubbling to the surface. "I know it sounds insane, but I was there. I saw it with my own eyes."

Rachel paced the room, her mind reeling. *This can't be happening,* she thought, *not after everything we've been through.* She turned to face Reyes, her eyes brimming with tears.

"So what are you saying?" she asked, her voice barely above a whisper. "That my husband is dead? That he was some kind of... some kind of monster?"

Reyes shook her head. "I don't know what to think anymore," she admitted. "But I do know that something strange is going on, something that goes beyond anything we've ever seen before."

Rachel sank back onto the couch, her anger giving way to despair. She buried her face in her hands, her shoulders shaking with silent sobs.

Reyes watched her, feeling the weight of her own helplessness pressing down on her.

"I'm sorry," Reyes said, her voice soft. "I wish I had better news, but I promised you the truth, no matter how hard it might be to hear."

Rachel looked up, her eyes red and puffy. "What am I supposed to do now?" she asked, her voice breaking. "How am I supposed to go on, not knowing what happened to my husband?"

Reyes reached out, placing a tentative hand on Rachel's shoulder. "We keep searching," she said, her voice firm. "We don't give up, no matter how bizarre or impossible it might seem. We owe it to Mark, and to ourselves, to find the truth."

Rachel nodded, taking a shaky breath. She knew the road ahead would be long and painful, but with Reyes by her side, she felt a flicker of hope in the darkness. Together, they would unravel the mystery of Mark's disappearance, no matter where it might lead them.

Reyes stood up, her gaze fixed on the charred pamphlet sitting on Rachel's coffee table. The alien hieroglyphs seemed to mock her, taunting her with secrets just out of reach. She picked it up, running her fingers over the rough edges, a reminder of the fiery end she'd witnessed in Canada.

"I know it sounds insane," Reyes said, her voice low and steady. "But I know what I saw, and I won't rest until I figure out what the hell is going on."

Rachel looked up at her, a flicker of determination in her eyes. "I want to help," she said, standing up to face Reyes. "I can't just sit here and wait for answers. I need to do something, anything, to find out what happened to Mark."

Reyes hesitated, weighing the risks of involving a civilian in the investigation. But the look on Rachel's face, the raw desperation and fierce resolve, made her reconsider. She nodded, a hint of a smile tugging at the corners of her mouth.

"Alright, but we do this my way," Reyes said, her tone leaving no room for argument. "We follow the leads, no matter how weird or dangerous they might be. And if things get too hot, you back off and let me handle it. Deal?"

Rachel nodded, a flicker of hope in her eyes. "Deal."

Reyes tucked the pamphlet into her jacket pocket, a reminder of the bizarre mystery that lay ahead. She knew the road would be long and treacherous, but with Rachel by her side, she felt a renewed sense of purpose. Together, they would uncover the truth behind Mark's disappearance and the strange events in Canada, no matter the cost.

As they stepped out into the cold Connecticut night, Reyes felt a chill run down her spine. The world seemed to shift around her, the shadows deepening and the stars above taking on an eerie, otherworldly glow. She shook off the feeling, focusing on the task at hand. There was work to be done, and she'd be damned if she let anything stand in her way.

Reyes drove through the dark streets, her mind racing with the possibilities of what lay ahead. She glanced at Rachel in the passenger seat, the woman's face illuminated by the glow of the streetlights. "So, where do we start?" Rachel asked, her voice a mix of determination and trepidation.

"The pamphlet," Reyes replied, her eyes fixed on the road. "Those symbols, that language... it's our only lead. We need to find someone who can translate it, someone who knows about this kind of weird shit."

Rachel nodded, her fingers absently tracing the edges of the framed photo in her lap. "I might know someone," she said quietly. "A professor at the university. He's an expert in ancient languages and mythology. If anyone can make sense of this, it's him."

Reyes raised an eyebrow, a hint of skepticism in her voice. "You think he'll believe us? This isn't exactly your typical academic inquiry."

"He's not your typical academic," Rachel replied, a wry smile on her face. "Trust me, he's seen his fair share of strange things. And if he can't help us, he'll know someone who can."

Reyes nodded, a flicker of hope in her chest. It was a long shot, but it was better than nothing. She turned the car onto the highway, the city lights fading in the rearview mirror as they sped towards the unknown.

As the miles ticked by, the conversation turned to their shared pain, the losses that had brought them together. "I never thought I'd be here," Rachel said softly, her voice barely audible over the hum of the engine. "Chasing after my husband, trying to make sense of the impossible. It feels like a bad dream."

Reyes nodded, her grip tightening on the steering wheel. "I know what you mean," she said, her voice rough with emotion. "When I lost my partner, I thought I'd never recover. The pain, the anger... it consumed me. But I had to keep going, had to find a way to make it mean something."

Rachel turned to face her, tears glistening in her eyes. "How did you do it? How did you keep going?"

Reyes was silent for a moment, the memories flooding back. "I focused on the job," she said finally, her voice steady. "I poured everything I had into my cases, into bringing justice to those who needed it. It didn't make the pain go away, but it gave me a reason to keep fighting."

Rachel nodded, her expression thoughtful. "I don't know if I have that kind of strength," she admitted, her voice barely a whisper.

Reyes reached over, her hand finding Rachel's in the darkness. "You do," she said firmly, her eyes locked on the road ahead. "You're here, aren't you? You're fighting for the truth, for your husband. That takes strength, more than you know."

Rachel squeezed her hand, a silent acknowledgment of the bond they shared. They drove on through the night, two women united by loss and determined to uncover the truth, no matter where it led them.

As the afternoon light faded, Reyes stood to leave, the weight of their conversation still heavy on her shoulders. She turned to Rachel, her voice low but resolute. "I won't give up on this, Rachel. I promise you, I'll keep searching for the truth, even if I have to do it alone."

Rachel looked up at her, a flicker of gratitude in her eyes amidst the pain and exhaustion. She nodded, her voice barely above a whisper. "Thank you, Detective. For everything."

Reyes managed a tight smile, the sincerity in Rachel's words touching a part of her she'd long kept guarded. She made her way to the door, the click of her boots against the hardwood floor echoing in the stillness of the house.

The chill of the evening air hit her as she stepped outside, a stark reminder of the cold reality she faced. She pulled her jacket tighter around her, her breath forming small clouds in the fading light. The walk to her car seemed longer than usual, each step weighted with the burden of the case that refused to let her go.

She slid into the driver's seat, the familiar scent of worn leather and stale coffee enveloping her. For a moment, she simply sat there, her hands gripping the steering wheel as her mind raced with the possibilities of what lay ahead. The charred pamphlet, the bizarre events in Canada, the missing husband - all pieces of a puzzle that seemed to defy logic and reason.

But Reyes had never been one to back down from a challenge. She'd faced her fair share of impossible cases, had stared down the barrel of a gun more times than she cared to remember. This was just another mystery to unravel, another truth to uncover.

She turned the key in the ignition, the engine roaring to life. As she pulled away from the curb, she caught a glimpse of Rachel in the rearview mirror, a solitary figure standing in the doorway, her arms

THE HUSBAND 121

wrapped tightly around herself. Reyes felt a pang of sympathy, a shared understanding of the pain that came with loss and betrayal.

But there was no time for sentiment, not now. She had a job to do, a promise to keep. She drove into the gathering darkness, her mind already racing with the next steps, the next leads to follow. The truth was out there, waiting to be found, and Reyes was determined to uncover it, no matter how bizarre or impossible it might seem.

The apartment was a mess, a testament to the chaos that had become Reyes's life. Takeout containers and empty coffee cups littered the desk, mingling with the scattered files and hastily scribbled notes. She slumped into her chair, the weight of the day settling heavily on her shoulders.

Her gaze fell on the charred pamphlet, its edges curled and blackened, the once-glossy surface now marred by soot and ash. She picked it up gingerly, her fingers tracing the alien hieroglyphs that seemed to mock her with their indecipherable secrets.

"What the hell are you trying to tell me?" she muttered, her brow furrowed in concentration.

She'd spent hours poring over the symbols, searching for patterns, for meaning in the madness. But every lead had proven fruitless, every theory more outlandish than the last.

Reyes leaned back in her chair, her eyes drifting to the ceiling. "Come on, Reyes," she said to herself, her voice a mix of frustration and determination. "You've cracked tougher cases than this. Think."

She closed her eyes, her mind replaying the events in Canada for the umpteenth time. The confrontation with the three Marks, the inexplicable language, the fiery end that had left more questions than answers.

"There's got to be a connection," she murmured, her fingers drumming restlessly on the desk. "Something we're missing."

She sat up suddenly, her eyes wide with realization. She grabbed a pen and began scribbling furiously on a notepad, her hand struggling to keep pace with her racing thoughts.

"The language," she said, her voice rising with excitement. "It's not just random symbols. It's a code."

She worked feverishly, her mind spinning with possibilities as she tried to decipher the alien script. Hours passed, the night bleeding into early morning, but Reyes barely noticed, her focus unwavering.

Finally, as the first rays of dawn began to filter through the blinds, she sat back, a triumphant grin spreading across her face.

"Gotcha," she said, holding up the notepad like a trophy. "Now let's see what secrets you've been hiding."

She knew it was just the beginning, that the road ahead would be long and treacherous. But for the first time since the case had landed on her desk, Reyes felt a flicker of hope, a glimmer of possibility.

She stood up, stretching her aching muscles, her mind already racing with the next steps. She had a lead, a direction, and a renewed sense of purpose.

"Alright, you bastards," she said, her voice a low growl. "Let's see what you're really up to."

With a final glance at the decoded message, Reyes grabbed her jacket and headed for the door, ready to face whatever lay ahead. The truth was out there, waiting to be uncovered, and she would stop at nothing to find it.

Reyes shuffled through the stack of case files littering her desk, the musty smell of old paperwork filling her nostrils. She leaned back in her creaky chair, rubbing her tired eyes. The phone's shrill ring pierced the air, jolting her from her thoughts. With a heavy sigh, she snatched up the receiver.

"Reyes Investigations," she answered flatly, expecting another desperate plea for help finding a lost cat or cheating spouse.

THE HUSBAND

The office door burst open, slamming against the wall. A middle-aged man stumbled in, his eyes wide with panic. Reyes jumped up, hand instinctively reaching for the pistol holstered at her hip.

"Whoa there, buddy. Take it easy," she warned, eyeing the disheveled stranger warily.

The man ran a shaky hand through his thinning hair. "Detective Reyes? I...I'm Tom. Tom Walker. I need your help. Something impossible just happened..."

Reyes gestured for him to sit, then leaned against the edge of her desk, arms crossed. "Alright, I'm listening. What's got you so spooked?"

Tom collapsed into the chair, wringing his trembling hands. "I saw myself. In the grocery store. I mean, it looked exactly like me, but it wasn't me. I...I think it was my doppelganger."

"Your doppelganger?" Reyes arched an eyebrow skeptically. But deep down, a flicker of curiosity ignited. She'd heard whispers of strange phenomena, unexplainable occurrences. Could this be connected? "Start from the beginning, Tom. Tell me everything."

As Tom dove into his bizarre tale, Reyes found herself leaning in, her mind racing with possibilities. This was no ordinary case. She could feel it in her bones. Something big was unfolding, and somehow, she'd landed smack in the middle of it.

Fuck, Reyes thought, this might just be the case I've been waiting for. Time to either prove I'm the real deal...or lose my damn mind trying.

Across town, Rachel Jennings sat hunched over a worn photo album, fingers tracing the smiling faces of her husband and daughter. She paused on a picture from last year's Fourth of July barbecue, Mark's arm slung casually around her shoulders, his grin wide and carefree.

But the longer Rachel stared, the more unsettled she felt. Something about Mark's smile seemed...off. Almost like it belonged to a stranger wearing her husband's skin.

"Get a grip, Rach," she muttered, snapping the album shut. "You're just seeing things."

Rachel pushed to her feet, joints popping in protest. She needed a distraction, something to quieten the nagging feeling that everything was about to unravel.

In the kitchen, she busied herself with mindless tasks—washing dishes, wiping counters, rearranging the magnets on the fridge. Anything to keep her hands busy and her mind occupied.

But even as she worked, Rachel couldn't shake the image of Mark's smile. The wrongness of it. Like a glitch in the fabric of reality.

Fuck, maybe I am losing it, she thought bleakly. First Mark disappears, then I start seeing things that aren't there.

Rachel braced herself against the counter, suddenly lightheaded. The weight of her grief, her confusion, threatened to crush her. She needed answers, needed to know what really happened to Mark.

Before she drowned in the not knowing.

The shrill buzz of her phone jolted Rachel out of her spiraling thoughts. She fumbled for the device, heart hammering against her ribs. Unknown number.

Rachel hesitated, thumb hovering over the screen. Probably just another scammer or telemarketer. She should let it go to voicemail, focus on keeping her shit together.

But something compelled her to answer. A tug in her gut, a whisper in her ear. "H-hello?"

Silence on the other end. Then, a rasp of static. "The truth is closer than you think."

Rachel's blood turned to ice. "Who is this? What the hell are you talking about?"

Click. The line went dead.

With shaking hands, Rachel lowered the phone. The cryptic message echoed in her mind, taunting her. Was it a prank? Some sick joke preying on her vulnerability?

Or was it something more sinister?

Rachel shivered, hugging herself tightly. She couldn't shake the feeling that the call was connected to Mark's disappearance. That whoever was on the other end knew more than they were letting on.

But how? And why reach out now, after all this time?

Frustrated, Rachel shoved her phone into her pocket. She needed to clear her head, get some fresh air. Maybe a walk would help settle her nerves.

As she reached for her keys, Rachel caught a glimpse of her reflection in the hall mirror. Pale skin, dark circles under her eyes. A woman on the edge.

She barely recognized herself anymore.

Across town, Reyes hunched over her desk, brow furrowed in concentration. Tom's file lay open before her, the pages covered in scribbled notes and question marks.

A doppelgänger sighting. It sounded like something out of a bad sci-fi movie. And yet, Tom had seemed so convinced, so shaken by the encounter.

Reyes tapped her pen against the desk, mind racing. Could there be a connection between Tom's case and the Jennings disappearance? At first glance, they seemed unrelated.

But the more she dug, the more parallels emerged. A sense of something not quite right. Details that didn't add up.

Reyes pulled the Jennings file closer, flipping through the pages. Mark's disappearance had been ruled an accident, his body never recovered. But what if there was more to the story?

What if, like Tom, Mark had encountered something he couldn't explain?

A chill raced down Reyes' spine. She was onto something, she could feel it in her bones. But what? Some sort of glitch in reality? A tear in the fabric of space and time?

Reyes shook her head, scoffing. Listen to yourself. You sound like a bad episode of The Twilight Zone.

And yet, she couldn't let it go. Couldn't ignore the nagging sense that she was on the verge of uncovering something big. Something that defied rational explanation.

Reyes leaned back in her chair, rubbing her temples. She needed answers, needed to make sense of the impossible. And to do that, she'd have to dig deeper.

Into quantum theories. Parallel universes. The nature of reality itself.

It was a daunting prospect, but Reyes had never been one to back down from a challenge. She'd follow this rabbit hole as far as it went.

Even if it meant losing herself along the way.

The hallowed halls of academia had never been Reyes' scene, but desperate times called for desperate measures. She strode through the physics department, her boots echoing on the polished floors, until she found the office she was looking for.

Dr. Patel, the nameplate read. Quantum Physics.

Reyes rapped her knuckles against the door, half-hoping the professor wouldn't be in. No such luck.

"Come in," a voice called from within.

Reyes pushed open the door, stepping into a cluttered office that looked like something out of a mad scientist's lab. Whiteboards covered in incomprehensible equations, stacks of books teetering on every surface, and in the midst of it all, a diminutive woman with a shock of silver hair.

"Dr. Patel?" Reyes ventured.

The woman looked up, peering at Reyes over the rims of her glasses. "That's me. And you are?"

"Alyssa Reyes. Private investigator." Reyes extended a hand, which Dr. Patel shook with a firm grip.

"What can I do for you, Ms. Reyes?"

Reyes hesitated, suddenly feeling foolish. "This is going to sound crazy, but... I've been investigating some cases that seem to involve, well, parallel universes."

Dr. Patel's eyebrows shot up. "Parallel universes, you say? Tell me more."

As Reyes launched into an explanation of Tom's doppelgänger sighting and the strange similarities to the Jennings case, Dr. Patel listened intently, her expression morphing from skeptical to intrigued.

"...and I know it sounds insane," Reyes finished, "but I can't shake the feeling that there's something to this. Something beyond our understanding of reality."

Dr. Patel leaned back in her chair, steepling her fingers. "What you're describing is consistent with certain multiverse theories. The idea that there are infinite parallel universes, each one slightly different from our own."

Reyes felt a surge of excitement. "So it's possible? That someone could cross over from one universe to another?"

"Theoretically, yes. But the amount of energy required would be staggering. And the consequences..." Dr. Patel shook her head. "Let's just say it's not something to be taken lightly."

Reyes' mind raced with the implications. If people were crossing over from other universes, what did that mean for their own reality? For the very nature of existence?

Meanwhile, across town, Rachel Jennings walked through her neighborhood, lost in thought. The cryptic message on her phone weighed heavily on her mind, a constant reminder of the questions that haunted her.

The truth is closer than you think.

But what truth? And how close was it?

Rachel turned a corner, her feet moving on autopilot, when a sudden flash of déjà vu stopped her in her tracks. A car passed by, and for a split second, she could have sworn she saw a familiar face behind the wheel.

Mark's face.

But that was impossible. Mark was gone, vanished without a trace. This had to be her mind playing tricks on her, conjuring ghosts from her past.

Rachel shook her head, trying to clear the cobwebs. She was losing it, that much was clear. Seeing things that couldn't possibly be real.

And yet, a small part of her wondered... what if?

What if the impossible was possible? What if the truth really was closer than she thought?

Rachel quickened her pace, a new sense of purpose filling her. She didn't know where this path would lead, but she knew she had to follow it.

No matter the cost.

Reyes burst into her office, her mind still reeling from the conversation with Dr. Patel. The implications of his theories were staggering, and she couldn't help but wonder if she was on the verge of something truly groundbreaking.

She was so lost in thought that she almost didn't notice the young woman sitting in the chair opposite her desk. Reyes blinked, taking in the woman's tear-stained face and trembling hands.

"Can I help you?" Reyes asked, her voice gentle.

The woman looked up, her eyes wide and haunted. "My name is Lisa," she said, her voice barely above a whisper. "I... I think I'm losing my mind."

Reyes sat down, leaning forward. "Why do you say that?"

Lisa took a shaky breath. "I saw my brother yesterday. But that's impossible because he... he died two years ago."

Reyes felt a chill run down her spine. Another one. Another case of someone seeing the impossible.

"Tell me everything," she said, grabbing a pen and notepad.

As Lisa recounted her story, Reyes listened intently, jotting down notes and asking questions. The details were eerily similar to the other cases she'd been investigating—a loved one, long dead, suddenly appearing out of nowhere.

But there was something else, too. A common thread that Reyes had overlooked until now.

"Lisa," she said, her voice urgent. "This is going to sound strange, but bear with me. Before you saw your brother, did you experience anything unusual? A strange dream, or a feeling of déjà vu?"

Lisa's eyes widened. "How did you know?"

Reyes leaned back in her chair, her mind racing. It was all connected. The dreams, the déjà vu, the impossible sightings. It had to be.

"I think I know what's happening," she said, her voice barely above a whisper. "But I need to be sure."

She stood up, pacing the room. The pieces were falling into place, but there were still so many questions. So many unknowns.

"Parallel realities," she muttered, more to herself than to Lisa. "Intersecting timelines. It's the only explanation."

Lisa looked at her, confusion etched on her face. "What are you talking about?"

Reyes turned to her, a fire in her eyes. "I think your brother is alive, Lisa. But not in this reality. In another one, running parallel to our own."

Lisa's mouth fell open. "That's... that's impossible."

"Is it?" Reyes asked, a hint of a smile on her face. "Think about it. The dreams, the déjà vu... it's like our minds are trying to tell us something. Like they're glimpsing into these other realities, even if only for a moment."

Lisa shook her head, trying to wrap her mind around it all. "But why? Why is this happening?"

Reyes sighed, running a hand through her hair. "That's what I need to find out. But one thing's for sure—I'm not going to rest until I get to the bottom of this."

She turned to Lisa, her expression softening. "I know it's a lot to take in. But I promise you, I will do everything in my power to find out the truth. For you, and for everyone else who's experienced something like this."

Lisa nodded, a glimmer of hope in her eyes. "Thank you," she whispered.

Reyes smiled, feeling a renewed sense of purpose. She was on the brink of something big, she could feel it in her bones.

And no matter what it took, she was going to see it through to the end.

Rachel stood at the river's edge, her eyes fixed on the murky water that had swallowed her husband whole. The memories came in waves, crashing against the shore of her mind like the relentless current before her.

She saw Mark's face, his smile, the way his eyes crinkled at the corners when he laughed. But then the image shifted, distorted, and suddenly it wasn't Mark at all. It was a stranger wearing his skin, a doppelgänger with a smile that didn't quite fit.

"What the hell is happening to me?" Rachel whispered, her voice carried away by the wind.

She closed her eyes, trying to separate the real from the imagined. But the more she grasped at the memories, the more they seemed to slip through her fingers like sand.

A twig snapped behind her, and Rachel whirled around, her heart pounding in her chest. But there was no one there. Just the trees and the shadows and the suffocating silence.

She turned back to the river, her reflection staring back at her from the water's surface. But was it really her? Or was it another version of herself, living a different life in a different world?

The thought made her head spin, and she stumbled back from the river's edge, her breath coming in short, sharp gasps.

"I'm losing my mind," she muttered, pressing her palms against her temples. "I'm fucking losing it."

But deep down, she knew it was more than that. Something was happening, something that defied explanation. And she was going to find out what it was, even if it meant confronting the truth she feared most.

Reyes pored over the files scattered across her desk, her brow furrowed in concentration. The cases were piling up, each one more bizarre than the last.

Missing persons, doppelgängers, inexplicable coincidences... it was like a cosmic jigsaw puzzle, and she was determined to piece it together.

She reached for her notebook, flipping through the pages of scribbled notes and half-formed theories. There had to be a pattern, a connection that tied it all together.

Her eyes landed on a name: Dr. Amelia Chen, a quantum physicist from San Francisco. She'd written a paper on parallel universes, and Reyes had a hunch she might be able to shed some light on the situation.

She grabbed her phone, dialing the number she'd jotted down. It rang once, twice, three times before a woman's voice answered.

"Dr. Chen speaking."

"Dr. Chen, my name is Detective Reyes. I'm investigating a series of unusual cases, and I was hoping you might be able to help me."

There was a pause on the other end of the line. "What kind of cases?"

Reyes took a deep breath. "Cases involving possible cross-overs between parallel realities."

Another pause, longer this time. "I see," Dr. Chen said slowly. "And what makes you think I can help?"

"Your research," Reyes replied. "I've read your paper on quantum entanglement and the multiverse theory. I think it might be related to what I'm seeing."

Dr. Chen sighed. "Detective, I appreciate your interest, but my work is purely theoretical. I can't help you with an active investigation."

Reyes's grip tightened on the phone. "Please, Dr. Chen. I'm at a dead end here. I need someone who understands this stuff, someone who can help me make sense of it all."

There was a long silence, and for a moment Reyes thought the line had gone dead. But then Dr. Chen spoke again, her voice low and cautious.

"Alright, Detective. I'll take a look at your cases. But I can't promise anything."

Reyes let out a breath she didn't realize she'd been holding. "Thank you, Dr. Chen. I'll send you the files right away."

She hung up the phone, feeling a surge of adrenaline coursing through her veins. Finally, a lead. A glimmer of hope in the darkness.

She turned back to her files, her mind racing with possibilities. She was close, she could feel it. Close to unraveling the mystery that had consumed her for so long.

And she wasn't going to stop until she had the truth, no matter where it led her.

Rachel stepped into her living room and froze, her heart slamming against her ribcage. The furniture had been rearranged—the couch pushed against the far wall, the coffee table turned at an odd angle, and the armchair facing the window instead of the TV. She blinked, trying to remember if she'd moved things around in a sleepwalking haze, but her mind drew a blank.

"What the hell?" she muttered, running a trembling hand through her hair. The room felt foreign, as if someone had invaded her sanctuary and left their mark.

She walked over to the bookshelf, her fingers tracing the spines of the novels she'd collected over the years. They were in the wrong order, alphabetized by author instead of title. A chill raced down her spine. She always arranged her books by title, a quirk she'd picked up in college.

Rachel sank onto the couch, her legs suddenly weak. Was she losing her mind? First the strange dreams, then the cryptic messages, and now this. She closed her eyes, trying to steady her breathing, but the room seemed to spin around her.

"Get a grip, Rach," she whispered to herself. "There has to be a logical explanation."

But even as the words left her lips, she knew there was nothing logical about any of this. Something was happening to her, something she couldn't explain or control.

She reached for her phone, her fingers hovering over the keypad. She needed to call someone, to tell them what was happening. But who would believe her? She could barely believe it herself.

Across town, Reyes's phone buzzed with an incoming message. She glanced at the screen, her brow furrowing at the unknown number.

"If you want answers, come to the old warehouse on 5th Street. Midnight. Come alone."

Reyes read the message twice, her pulse quickening. It could be a trap, a setup by someone trying to derail her investigation. But something in her gut told her this was the real deal.

She glanced at the clock. She had four hours until midnight. Four hours to prepare, to arm herself with whatever she might need.

She stood up, grabbing her jacket from the back of her chair. She had a feeling she was about to step into something bigger than herself, something that would change everything she thought she knew.

But she was ready. Ready to face whatever lay ahead, ready to uncover the truth, no matter the cost.

Reyes spent the next few hours in a frenzy of preparation. She pored over the case files, searching for any clue or connection she might have missed. She made a list of questions, of theories to explore, of leads to follow up on.

But as midnight approached, she found herself growing more and more anxious. She checked and double-checked her gun, making sure it was loaded and ready. She slipped a knife into her boot, a taser into her pocket.

She knew the risks. Knew that walking into that warehouse alone was a gamble, a roll of the dice with her life on the line. But she also knew that this was her chance, her one shot at getting to the bottom of this mystery.

At 11:45, she climbed into her car and headed for the warehouse district. The streets were empty, the only sound the hum of her engine and the pounding of her heart.

She parked a block away, taking a moment to steady her nerves. She could feel the adrenaline pumping through her veins, the electric thrill of anticipation.

She checked her watch. 11:59. It was time.

She stepped out of the car, the cool night air hitting her face like a slap. She took a deep breath, steeling herself for whatever lay ahead.

And then she walked, her footsteps echoing off the pavement as she made her way towards the warehouse. Towards answers, towards the truth, towards a future she couldn't even begin to imagine.

As she approached the door, she saw a figure step out of the shadows. A man, tall and lean, his face obscured by a hood.

"Detective Reyes," he said, his voice low and gravelly. "I've been expecting you."

Reyes's hand tightened on her gun, her heart hammering in her chest. This was it. The moment of truth.

She stepped forward, ready to face whatever lay ahead. Ready to finally uncover the secrets that had been haunting her for so long.

THE HUSBAND

And as she followed the man into the darkness of the warehouse, she knew there was no turning back. The game was on, and she was all in.

Reyes burst through the door of the cluttered apartment, a charred pamphlet clenched in her fist. The stench of stale pizza and unwashed laundry assaulted her nostrils. Amid the chaos of scattered papers and flickering computer monitors hunched Alex, oblivious to her dramatic entrance.

"Alex, you lazy sonofabitch, I need you to take a look at this. Now." Reyes slapped the singed paper down on the desk, scattering empty soda cans.

Alex looked up, blinking owlishly behind thick glasses. "Well hello to you too, Sunshine. To what do I owe the pleasure of your delightful company today?" His voice dripped with sarcasm.

"Cut the crap. This pamphlet turned up at a crime scene. I need it deciphered yesterday." Reyes jabbed a finger at the strange symbols, her patience already stretched gossamer thin. Every second wasted was another second for the perp to slip away.

Adjusting his glasses, Alex snatched up the paper and squinted at the alien markings. "Huh. Looks like some kinda code. Gimme a sec." His fingers flew over the keyboard, pulling up obscure databases and algorithms.

Reyes paced behind him, her black boots crunching on discarded potato chip bags. This was a dead end. Had to be. No way some nutjob's coded diary was going to crack this case. But her gut insisted otherwise, an itch she couldn't scratch.

Alex muttered to himself as he worked, a mad scientist lost in his element. Symbols flashed across the screen in an epileptic lightshow. "C'mon you bastard, give it up already..."

Reyes clenched her jaw, resisting the urge to put her fist through the drywall. Every instinct screamed at her to get back on the streets, to hunt, to end this. But she forced herself to wait, to trust Alex's process, fucked as it was.

Because if anyone could make sense of this mess, it was him. God help them all.

The minutes dragged by, each one an eternity. Reyes couldn't shake the feeling that this pamphlet, this meaningless scrap of paper, held the key to unraveling the whole damn mystery. Mark Jennings. The man who wouldn't stay dead. The ghost haunting her every waking moment.

She'd seen him die, watched the light fade from his eyes. And yet, there he was, week after week, caught on camera, strolling through the city like he owned the place. It defied logic, reason, everything she knew to be true.

But if there was one thing Reyes had learned in this line of work, it was that the truth didn't give a shit about logic.

The room buzzed with the hum of computers, the clacking of keys, and the occasional "fuck" from Alex as he hit another dead end. Reyes leaned over his shoulder, her eyes scanning the gibberish on the screen, praying for a breakthrough.

"There's gotta be something, Alex. This can't be another fucking goose chase." Her voice was low, tight with frustration.

Alex didn't look up, his fingers never slowing their dance. "I'm trying, Rey. This shit's not exactly my usual Saturday night, ya know?"

Reyes snorted. "What, you mean you don't spend your weekends elbow-deep in Zodiac Killer fan fiction?"

"Nah, I prefer the Unabomber. Better fashion sense."

Despite herself, Reyes cracked a smile. Leave it to Alex to find the humor in this twisted situation. God knew she needed it. Needed something to cut through the fog of obsession and confusion that had consumed her life.

She turned back to the screen, her brief moment of levity fading as quickly as it had come. The symbols seemed to mock her, daring her to unravel their secrets.

But Reyes had never been one to back down from a challenge. And she sure as hell wasn't about to start now.

Not when the truth was so close she could taste it.

"Holy shit, I think I've got something!" Alex's sudden shout pierced the tense silence, making Reyes jump.

She leaned in closer, her heart hammering against her ribs. "What is it? What did you find?"

Alex jabbed a finger at the screen, his eyes wide behind his glasses. "This fragment here, it's talking about some kind of cosmic experiment. Something to do with parallel realities."

Reyes felt a chill race down her spine. Parallel realities? The concept was like something out of a sci-fi novel, but after everything she'd seen, she was starting to believe that anything was possible.

"Fuck me," she breathed, her mind reeling with the implications. "Are you telling me that Mark Jennings is mixed up in some kind of interdimensional fuckery?"

Alex shrugged, his fingers already flying across the keyboard again. "I don't know, but it sure as hell looks that way. This fragment suggests that the experiment was designed to manipulate the fabric of reality itself."

Reyes felt a wave of vertigo wash over her. The idea was too vast, too mind-bending to comprehend. How could Mark, the man she'd known for years, be involved in something so grandiose? So utterly insane?

She stumbled back a step, bracing herself against the edge of the desk. "This can't be real. It's gotta be some kind of joke, right? A prank?"

But even as the words left her mouth, she knew they weren't true. The charred edges of the pamphlet, the alien symbols that danced before her eyes - it was all too elaborate, too fucking weird to be a hoax.

No, this was real. And it was bigger than anything she could have ever imagined.

Reyes took a deep breath, trying to steady herself. She couldn't afford to fall apart now. Not when she was so close to the truth.

She leaned forward again, her eyes locked on the screen. "Okay, so what else does it say? What's the endgame here?"

Alex shook his head, his brow furrowed in concentration. "I'm not sure yet. The rest of the fragment is even more cryptic. But I've got a feeling we're just scratching the surface of this thing."

Reyes nodded, her jaw clenched tight. She knew he was right. Whatever this was, it was big. Bigger than her, bigger than Mark, bigger than anything she'd ever faced before.

But she'd be damned if she was going to let that stop her.

She was Reyes fucking Calderon, and she never backed down from a fight.

Even if that fight was against the very fabric of reality itself.

Reyes watched as Alex's fingers flew across the keyboard, his eyes darting from screen to screen as he decoded the next fragment. The room was silent save for the hum of the computers and the occasional muttered curse from Alex as he hit a particularly tough section.

She paced the room, her mind racing with the implications of what they'd uncovered so far. Mark Jennings, the man she'd been chasing for months, was no mere criminal mastermind.

Reyes' mind flashed back to the bizarre sightings and inexplicable events surrounding Mark's case. The witnesses who swore they'd seen him in two places at once, the impossible escapes, the way he seemed to vanish into thin air. It all started to make a twisted kind of sense.

"Holy shit," Alex breathed, his eyes wide as he stared at the screen. "This is... this is next level stuff, Reyes."

She leaned over his shoulder, her heart pounding as she read the decoded text. It spoke of alternate timelines, of parallel realities bleeding into one another, of a grand experiment orchestrated by a mind far beyond anything they could comprehend.

And at the center of it all, pulling the strings like some kind of demented puppet master, was Mark Jennings.

Reyes felt a chill run down her spine, a mixture of awe and dread that left her breathless. She'd always known there was something off about Mark, something that didn't quite add up. But this? This was beyond anything she could have imagined.

"Keep going," she said, her voice barely above a whisper. "We need to know everything."

Alex nodded, his fingers already flying across the keyboard again. Each new fragment he decoded added another layer to the mystery, another piece to the impossible puzzle they found themselves trapped in.

Reyes felt like she was standing on the edge of a precipice, staring down into an abyss of secrets and lies that threatened to swallow her whole. But she couldn't back down now. Not when they were so close to the truth.

No matter how terrifying that truth might be.

The room crackled with an electric tension as Alex worked, his brow furrowed in concentration. Reyes paced behind him, her mind racing with the implications of what they'd uncovered.

"Holy shit," Alex muttered, his eyes widening as he deciphered a particularly cryptic passage. "Reyes, you need to see this."

She leaned in, her pulse quickening as she read the words on the screen. The passage hinted at the ongoing nature of the experiment, suggesting that it was far from over. That the boundaries between realities were growing thinner by the day, and that soon, the very fabric of the universe itself might begin to unravel.

"What the fuck does that mean?" Reyes asked, her voice trembling slightly.

Alex shook his head, his expression grim. "It means we're in deep shit, Reyes. Deeper than we ever could have imagined."

Reyes felt a wave of dread wash over her, a sinking feeling in the pit of her stomach. She'd always known that the truth would be hard to swallow, but this? This was beyond anything she'd been prepared for.

But even as the fear threatened to overwhelm her, Reyes felt a flicker of determination spark to life in her chest. She'd come too far to back down now, too far to let the truth slip through her fingers.

No matter how ugly that truth might be, she had to see it through to the end.

"Keep digging," she said, her voice steady despite the tremor in her hands. "We need to know everything, Alex. Every last fucking detail."

He nodded, turning back to the screen with a renewed sense of urgency. Reyes watched him work, her mind spinning with the possibilities of what they might uncover next.

She knew they were standing on the brink of something monumental, something that could change the course of history itself. And as terrifying as that thought was, Reyes couldn't help but feel a thrill of excitement coursing through her veins.

The truth was out there, waiting to be discovered. And come hell or high water, she was going to find it.

Reyes paced the cramped room, her mind a whirlwind of theories and speculation. The implications of the decoded fragments were staggering, hinting at a cosmic conspiracy that seemed too far-fetched to be true. And yet, the evidence was right there in front of her, undeniable and impossible to ignore.

She glanced at the photo of Mark Jennings pinned to the corkboard, his enigmatic smile taunting her from across the room. What was his role in all of this? Was he the mastermind behind the experiment, pulling the strings from some hidden location? Or was he just another pawn, a helpless victim caught up in a game he didn't understand?

The uncertainty gnawed at Reyes, fueling her determination to unravel the mystery once and for all. She had to know the truth, no matter how painful or shocking it might be.

"Holy shit," Alex muttered, his eyes widening as he stared at the screen. "You're not gonna believe this."

Reyes whirled around, her heart pounding in her chest. "What is it? What did you find?"

Alex pointed to a line of text, his finger trembling slightly. "It says here that the experiment is still ongoing. That it never ended, even after all these years."

The revelation hit Reyes like a punch to the gut, leaving her breathless and reeling. She gripped the edge of the desk, her knuckles turning white as she struggled to process the implications of Alex's words.

"But that means..." she trailed off, her mind racing with the possibilities.

"That we're all still part of it," Alex finished, his voice barely above a whisper. "That everything we've experienced, everything we've been through, it's all been part of the experiment from the very beginning."

Reyes felt like the ground was shifting beneath her feet, like reality itself was unraveling around her. The thought that her entire life might have been manipulated, that every choice she'd ever made might have been predetermined by some unseen force, was almost too much to bear.

But even as the fear threatened to overwhelm her, Reyes knew she couldn't give up. Not now, not when she was so close to the truth.

She straightened her shoulders, her jaw set with determination. "Then we keep digging," she said, her voice steady despite the tremor in her hands. "We don't stop until we have all the answers, no matter where they lead us."

Alex nodded, a fierce glint in his eyes. "Let's do this."

Reyes' eyes locked onto the decoded text, her mind a whirlwind of possibilities and fears. The cryptic symbols seemed to dance before her eyes, taunting her with their hidden meanings. She knew she had to act fast, but the path forward was shrouded in uncertainty and danger.

"This is some seriously messed up shit," Reyes muttered, running a hand through her disheveled hair. "If what you're saying is true, Alex, then we're dealing with something way bigger than just Mark Jennings."

Alex leaned back in his chair, his eyes flickering between the screen and Reyes. "You're not wrong, Rey. This experiment, whatever it is, it's not just about one man. It's about the nature of reality itself."

Reyes began to pace the cluttered room, her mind racing with the implications. If the experiment was ongoing, then who was behind it? And what was their endgame? The thought of being a pawn in some cosmic game made her blood boil.

"We need to find out who's pulling the strings," she said, her voice low and determined. "And we need to put a stop to it, before it's too late."

Alex nodded, his fingers already flying across the keyboard. "I'll keep digging, see if I can find any more clues in the decoded fragments. But Reyes, you need to be careful out there. If this experiment is as big as we think it is, then there's no telling who might be watching."

With a newfound sense of urgency, Reyes thanked Alex and gathered the decoded fragments, her mind already racing with plans for her next move. She knew the stakes were higher than ever, and failure was not an option.

As she stepped out into the cold night air, Reyes felt a chill run down her spine. The truth was out there, waiting to be uncovered, but she knew that every step she took would be fraught with danger. She took a deep breath, steeling herself for the battles to come.

"Game on, you bastards," she whispered to the shadows. "Game fucking on."

The city streets were a blur as Reyes tore through them, her mind still reeling from the revelations in Alex's lair. The decoded fragments felt like a lead weight in her pocket, a tangible reminder of the impossible truth she'd stumbled upon.

THE HUSBAND

"Parallel realities, cosmic experiments... it's all so fucking insane," she muttered to herself, shaking her head in disbelief.

But deep down, Reyes knew it was true. The bizarre sightings, the inexplicable events surrounding Mark Jennings' case... it all made a twisted kind of sense now. She couldn't shake the feeling that she was on the cusp of something world-shattering, something that would change everything she thought she knew.

As she wove through the late-night traffic, Reyes' thoughts drifted to Mark. Where was he now? Was he truly the mastermind behind this mind-bending experiment, or was he just another victim, caught up in forces beyond his control?

The questions churned in her gut, fueling her determination to unravel the mystery. She knew she couldn't do it alone, but who could she trust? In a world where reality itself was up for grabs, it was hard to know who was on her side.

Reyes' fingers tightened on the steering wheel as she made a sharp turn, her tires screeching against the pavement. The truth was out there, tantalizingly close yet maddeningly elusive, and she was determined to chase it down, no matter where it led.

"You can't hide forever, you sons of bitches," she growled, her eyes narrowing with resolve. "I'm coming for you, and heaven help anyone who tries to stop me."

As the city lights flickered past her windows, Reyes felt a surge of adrenaline coursing through her veins. The game was on, and she was ready to play. No matter how deep the rabbit hole went, no matter how dangerous the road ahead, she would stop at nothing to uncover the truth behind the cosmic experiment that had turned her world upside down.

The diner buzzed with chatter and clanking dishes, but the air between Detective Reyes and Rachel Jennings was thick with unspoken tension. Reyes slid a worn manila folder across the scuffed linoleum table, her voice low and steady. "I know it sounds crazy, but just look at the evidence. The sightings, the strange reports - it all points to something more than a typical missing persons case."

Rachel stared at the folder, her hands trembling slightly as she flipped it open. Photos and reports spilled out, each more bizarre than the last. Her eyes widened as she scanned the pages, her breath catching in her throat. This couldn't be real. Mark couldn't have just vanished into thin air.

She slammed the folder shut, her voice rising with each word. "Is this some kind of sick joke? You expect me to believe this bullshit?" She jabbed a finger at Reyes, her eyes flashing with anger. "You're just trying to cover your own ass because you can't find him. Admit it, you fucked up the investigation from the start."

Heads turned at nearby tables, curious eyes drawn by Rachel's outburst. Reyes leaned forward, her gaze unwavering. "Listen, I know how it sounds. But I've been doing this a long time, and I've never seen anything like it. Multiple witnesses, strange phenomena - it defies explanation."

Rachel shook her head, a bitter laugh escaping her lips. "Defies explanation? More like you're grasping at straws. Making up stories instead of doing your damn job."

She rifled through the photos again, her stomach churning at the blurry images. Mark's face, flickering and distorted. Impossible shadows. Her mind reeled, trying to make sense of it all.

"This is insane," she muttered, more to herself than to Reyes. "There has to be a logical explanation. Maybe he just...ran off. Had some kind of breakdown."

Even as the words left her mouth, Rachel knew they rang hollow. Mark wasn't the type to just disappear. And these photos, these reports - as much as she wanted to deny it, they pointed to something far stranger than a midlife crisis.

She looked up at Reyes, her anger giving way to a desperate, pleading edge. "So what now? You're the detective. Where do we go from here?"

Reyes met her gaze, a flicker of understanding passing between them. "We start at the beginning. Retrace his steps, talk to anyone who might have seen something. And we keep an open mind, no matter how crazy it seems."

Rachel nodded slowly, her fingers tightening around the edge of the folder. She knew deep down that Reyes was right. If she wanted answers, she'd have to be willing to follow the truth, wherever it led.

Even if it meant confronting the impossible.

Reyes leaned forward, her elbows resting on the table as she fixed Rachel with a steady gaze. "There's one more thing you need to know. A sighting that I didn't include in the official report."

Rachel's eyebrows shot up, her heart skipping a beat. "What? Why not?"

"Because it's the most bizarre of them all." Reyes paused, as if gathering her thoughts. "A few days ago, a hiker in Banff National Park, Canada, reported seeing a man who matched Mark's description. But here's the thing - the hiker claimed the man appeared and disappeared in the blink of an eye. Like he was flickering in and out of existence."

Rachel's mouth fell open, a chill running down her spine. "That's... that's not possible."

"I know how it sounds," Reyes said, her voice low and urgent. "But I spoke with the hiker myself. He was shaken, but he seemed lucid. And he was adamant about what he saw."

Rachel shook her head, trying to wrap her mind around the implications. "So, what are you saying? That Mark is somehow... teleporting?"

"I don't know what I'm saying," Reyes admitted. "But I do know that we can't ignore this. We need to go to these places - the park in

Canada, the kayak launch point, his old office. See if we can find any clues, any pattern to these sightings."

Rachel hesitated, fear and doubt warring with the desperate need for answers. She thought of Mark, of the life they'd built together, of the future that had been ripped away. And in that moment, she knew she'd do whatever it took to find him.

"Okay," she said, her voice barely above a whisper. "Let's do it. Let's go to Canada."

Reyes nodded, a glimmer of respect in her eyes. She signaled for the check, and as they walked out of the diner, Rachel felt a newfound sense of purpose. She didn't know what they would find, but for the first time since Mark's disappearance, she felt a flicker of hope.

Maybe, just maybe, they were one step closer to the truth.

The Jennings' suburban home loomed before them, a picture-perfect facade that belied the turmoil within. Rachel's hand trembled as she reached for the doorknob, the metal cold beneath her fingertips. She hesitated, her heart hammering against her ribcage as memories threatened to overwhelm her.

"You okay?" Reyes asked, her voice uncharacteristically gentle.

Rachel swallowed hard, steeling herself. "Yeah. Let's just... let's just get this over with."

She pushed the door open, the hinges creaking in protest. The air inside was stale, heavy with the weight of unspoken memories. Rachel stepped over the threshold, her footsteps echoing in the eerie stillness.

Family photos lined the hallway, frozen moments of happiness that now felt like a cruel mockery. Rachel's gaze lingered on a picture of her and Mark, their arms wrapped around each other, their smiles wide and carefree. She remembered the day it was taken, a lazy Sunday afternoon at the park. They'd been so happy then, so blissfully unaware of the darkness that lurked on the horizon.

"Rachel?" Reyes prompted, her voice cutting through the haze of memories.

Rachel shook herself, tearing her eyes away from the photo. "I'm fine. Let's keep moving."

They made their way through the house, the floorboards creaking beneath their feet. The air seemed to grow heavier with each step, the shadows deepening in the corners of the room. Rachel couldn't shake the feeling that they were being watched, that some unseen presence was lurking just out of sight.

Suddenly, the lights flickered, plunging them into momentary darkness. Rachel's breath caught in her throat, her heart racing. She reached for the wall, her fingers scrabbling for purchase as she tried to steady herself.

"What the hell was that?" Reyes muttered, her hand reaching for her gun.

Before Rachel could respond, a sound drifted through the air, a sound that sent chills down her spine. It was laughter, achingly familiar and yet impossibly out of place. Mark's laughter.

"Did you hear that?" Rachel whispered, her voice trembling.

Reyes nodded, her eyes narrowing. "Stay close. And keep your eyes open."

They moved deeper into the house, the laughter growing louder with each step. It seemed to come from everywhere and nowhere at once, a ghostly echo that defied explanation. Rachel's mind raced, trying to make sense of the impossible. Mark was gone, vanished without a trace. He couldn't be here, couldn't be laughing in the empty halls of their once-happy home.

And yet, the evidence was undeniable. The sightings, the strange phenomena, the cryptic warnings - it all pointed to something far beyond their understanding. Something that threatened to unravel the very fabric of reality.

Rachel's fingers curled into fists, a newfound determination taking root in her heart. She would find the truth, no matter the cost. For

Mark, for their life together, for the future that had been stolen from them.

She glanced at Reyes, saw the same resolve mirrored in the detective's eyes. They were in this together now, bound by the impossible and the inexplicable.

And as the laughter faded into the shadows, Rachel knew that their journey was only just beginning.

The next stop on their surreal odyssey was Mark's former workplace, a nondescript office building that seemed to loom ominously in the fading light. Rachel's heart hammered against her ribs as they approached the entrance, a sense of unease prickling along her spine.

"You ready for this?" Reyes asked, her hand resting on the door handle.

Rachel nodded, steeling herself. "As ready as I'll ever be."

They stepped inside, the air heavy with an unnatural stillness. The usual hum of activity was absent, replaced by an eerie silence that seemed to press in from all sides. Rachel's footsteps echoed too loudly on the polished floor, each sound a jarring intrusion in the oppressive quiet.

As they made their way through the labyrinth of cubicles, the computers flickered to life, their screens casting a sickly glow across the darkened space. Rachel froze, her breath catching in her throat as distorted images of Mark's face danced across the monitors, his features twisting and warping in a nightmarish kaleidoscope.

"What the hell is this?" she whispered, her voice trembling.

Reyes shook her head, her eyes narrowed. "I don't know. But I don't like it."

They pressed on, the images growing more disturbing with each passing moment. Mark's face contorted in silent screams, his eyes wide and pleading, as if begging for help from beyond the veil. Rachel's stomach churned, a cold sweat breaking out across her skin.

And then, as suddenly as they had appeared, the images vanished, plunging the office into darkness once more. Rachel let out a shaky breath, her heart racing.

"We need to keep moving," Reyes said, her voice low and urgent.

They left the office behind, the weight of the unseen pressing down on them like a physical force. The next stop was the riverbank where Mark's kayak had been found, a place that held a special sort of dread for Rachel.

As they approached the water's edge, Rachel felt a chill run through her, a bone-deep cold that had nothing to do with the temperature. The river flowed with an unnatural stillness, its surface as smooth and dark as obsidian.

She stood at the edge, her mind flashing back to the day Mark disappeared. The frantic search, the hope that had slowly dwindled to despair, the realization that he was truly gone. It all came rushing back, a tidal wave of grief and loss that threatened to pull her under.

Beside her, Reyes scanned the area, her eyes sharp and searching. "There's something off about this place," she muttered, her hand resting on her holster. "I can feel it."

Rachel nodded, the hairs on the back of her neck standing on end. The air seemed to hum with a strange energy, a palpable sense of wrongness that set her teeth on edge.

And as they stood there, staring out at the unnaturally still water, Rachel knew that they were on the precipice of something beyond their wildest imaginings. Something that would change everything, forever.

As Rachel's mind reeled with the impossible sight before her, a flickering apparition of Mark materialized on the opposite bank. His form was unstable, shifting like a mirage in the desert heat, and yet there was no denying it was him.

"What the fuck?" Rachel gasped, her instincts screaming at her to run, to get as far away from this unnatural phenomenon as possible.

But her feet remained rooted to the spot, her eyes locked on the ghostly figure of her husband.

Beside her, Reyes stood firm, her hand still resting on her holster. "Mark Jennings!" she called out, her voice ringing with authority. "We need answers. What the hell is going on here?"

The flickering Mark turned his head, his eyes locking with Rachel's. In that moment, she saw a depth of pain and desperation that took her breath away. "Rach," he whispered, his voice echoing with layers of sound that sent shivers down her spine. "You have to listen to me. Reality... it's unraveling. Everything we thought we knew... it's all wrong."

Rachel's heart pounded in her chest, her mind struggling to make sense of his words. "What are you talking about, Mark? What's happening to you?"

The apparition flickered, his form growing more unstable by the second. "There's no time," he urged, his words fragmented and distorted. "You have to find the truth. Before it's too late. Before everything falls apart."

Reyes stepped forward, her eyes narrowed. "What truth, Mark? What are we supposed to be looking for?"

But even as she spoke, the flickering Mark began to fade, his image dissolving into the air like smoke on the wind. "Find the key," he whispered, his voice barely audible over the rushing of the river. "Unlock the mystery. Before it's too late."

And then he was gone, leaving Rachel and Reyes standing alone on the riverbank, their minds reeling with questions and a growing sense of dread. What the hell had they just witnessed? And what did it mean for the investigation, for the world as they knew it?

Rachel turned to Reyes, her eyes wide with a mix of fear and determination. "We have to figure this out," she said, her voice shaking but resolute. "Whatever the hell is going on here, we can't let it go. We owe it to Mark, to ourselves, to get to the bottom of it."

THE HUSBAND

Reyes nodded, her jaw set with grim determination. "Damn straight," she agreed, her eyes scanning the riverbank for any clues left behind. "We're in this now, Rachel. And we're not stopping until we find the truth, no matter how fucking weird it gets."

Rachel drew a shaky breath, her mind spinning as she tried to process the impossibility of what they'd just witnessed. The flickering apparition of her husband, the cryptic warnings about reality unraveling—it defied every rational explanation she'd clung to for so long. Her skepticism, once an unshakable fortress, now crumbled under the weight of the evidence before her eyes.

"I don't know what to believe anymore," she whispered, her voice barely audible over the gentle lapping of the river. "Everything I thought I knew, everything I thought was real... it's all falling apart."

Reyes placed a firm hand on Rachel's shoulder, her gaze unwavering. "We can't let ourselves get lost in the doubts," she said, her voice steady and resolute. "We have to focus on the facts, on what we can see and touch and investigate. The answers are out there, Rachel. We just have to be strong enough to find them."

Rachel nodded, drawing strength from Reyes' conviction. She knew the detective was right—they couldn't afford to let the strangeness of the situation overwhelm them. They had to approach it like any other case, one step at a time, piecing together the clues until the truth emerged.

"So what's our next move?" Rachel asked, straightening her shoulders and meeting Reyes' gaze head-on.

Reyes cracked a wry smile. "We hit the books," she said, gesturing towards the car. "We go back to the station, dig through every damn file and report we can find. There's got to be a pattern, a connection we're missing. And we don't stop until we find it."

Rachel followed Reyes back to the car, her mind already racing with possibilities. The key, the mystery, the unraveling of reality—it all had to tie together somehow. And she was determined to find out how, no matter how deep down the rabbit hole she had to go.

As they drove away from the riverbank, the weight of the unknown pressed down on them both. But beneath it, a flicker of hope burned bright—the hope that, together, they could unlock the truth and bring Mark home, no matter how strange or impossible the journey might be.

The car rumbled down the winding road, the silence between Rachel and Reyes thick with unspoken thoughts. Rachel's fingers drummed against her thigh, a nervous energy coursing through her veins. She couldn't shake the image of Mark's flickering form, the cryptic warnings that echoed in her mind.

"You think we're in over our heads?" she asked, her voice barely audible over the hum of the engine.

Reyes glanced at her, a flicker of understanding in her eyes. "Probably," she admitted, her grip tightening on the steering wheel. "But when has that ever stopped us before?"

A wry chuckle escaped Rachel's lips. "Fair point." She leaned back in her seat, watching the trees blur past the window. "I just can't help feeling like we're on the edge of something big, you know? Like we're about to step into a world we don't fully understand."

Reyes nodded, her gaze fixed on the road ahead. "I know what you mean. But we've faced the unknown before, Rach. We've stared down the barrel of the impossible and come out the other side. This is just another mystery to unravel."

Rachel felt a surge of gratitude for the detective's unwavering resolve. She knew that, together, they could face whatever lay ahead. They had the skills, the determination, and most importantly, each other's backs.

As the car sped towards the city, Rachel's mind raced with the possibilities of what they might uncover. The flickering version of Mark, the strange phenomena, the unraveling of reality itself—it all pointed to something far greater than a simple missing persons case.

But she knew one thing for certain: she wouldn't rest until she found the truth. No matter how deep they had to dig, no matter what horrors they might face, she would stop at nothing to bring Mark home and unravel the mystery that had consumed their lives.

With a shared look of determination, Rachel and Reyes drove on, ready to plunge headfirst into the unknown and confront the truth, no matter the cost.

Reyes paced back and forth in her cluttered office, the alien pamphlet gripped tightly in her hand. Her eyes darted across the strange symbols and diagrams, her mind struggling to comprehend their meaning. The implications were staggering, world-changing. She glanced at the clock on the wall, its ticking suddenly louder in her ears. Only a few hours until her meeting with Rachel. Shit.

She tossed the pamphlet onto her desk, scattering papers and empty coffee cups. "This can't be real," she muttered, running a hand through her disheveled hair. But deep down, she knew it was. The evidence was right there, mocking her from the chaos of her workspace. She had to pull it together, figure out what the hell she was going to say to Rachel.

Reyes snatched her jacket from the back of her chair and headed for the door, her mind still reeling. She paused with her hand on the knob, taking a deep breath. "Here goes nothing," she said, stepping out into the unknown.

Across town, Rachel sat in her dimly lit living room, the silence broken only by the occasional creak of the old house settling. She was surrounded by photos of Mark, of their life together, now shattered into a million pieces. His smiling face stared back at her from every frame, a cruel reminder of all she had lost.

She clutched a cup of cold coffee, the once comforting aroma now stale and bitter. Her thoughts swirled in a chaotic mix of grief and confusion, questions with no answers. Why had Mark been taken from her? What was the meaning behind his cryptic final words?

Rachel's gaze fell on their wedding photo, their faces bright with love and promise. A sob caught in her throat as she traced a finger over Mark's image. "I don't know what to do," she whispered, her voice cracking. "I need you here. I need answers."

But there were no answers, only the suffocating weight of loss and the looming specter of the unknown. Rachel set her mug down with a shaky hand, steeling herself for Reyes' arrival. She had to be strong, had to find a way forward, even if it meant facing the unimaginable. For Mark, for their future that would never be, she had to try.

Reyes' car screeched to a halt in Rachel's driveway, the sudden silence deafening. She sat there for a moment, hands white-knuckled on the steering wheel, heart pounding against her ribs. This was it. The moment of truth.

She glanced at the alien pamphlet on the passenger seat, its strange symbols seeming to mock her. What the hell was she supposed to say? "Hey, Rachel, I think your husband might have been abducted by aliens from another universe"? Yeah, that would go over well.

Reyes took a deep breath, steeling herself. She had to do this. For Mark. For Rachel. For the whole damn world, if her suspicions were right.

She grabbed the pamphlet and shoved it into her jacket pocket, then climbed out of the car. The walk to Rachel's front door felt like a mile, each step heavy with the weight of what was to come.

Reyes raised her fist to knock, but the door swung open before she could make contact. Rachel stood there, her face pale and drawn, eyes red-rimmed from crying. She looked like hell, but there was a flicker of something in her gaze. Hope, maybe. Or desperation.

"Detective Reyes." Rachel's voice was hoarse, barely above a whisper. "Please, come in."

Reyes stepped inside, the tension in the air palpable and heavy. It pressed down on her like a physical weight, making it hard to breathe.

THE HUSBAND

She followed Rachel into the living room, taking in the clutter of photos and mementos, the half-empty coffee mug on the table.

Rachel sank onto the couch, looking up at Reyes with a mix of hope and skepticism. "You said you had some information about Mark's disappearance?"

Reyes nodded, perching on the edge of an armchair. She could feel the pamphlet burning a hole in her pocket, but she couldn't bring herself to pull it out. Not yet.

"I do," she said carefully. "But I need you to keep an open mind. What I'm about to tell you...it's going to sound crazy."

Rachel let out a brittle laugh. "Crazier than my husband vanishing into thin air? Try me."

Reyes took a deep breath, bracing herself. This was it. The point of no return. She reached into her pocket and pulled out the pamphlet, its alien symbols seeming to glow in the dim light.

"I think Mark's disappearance might be connected to something much bigger," she said, holding out the pamphlet. "Something that could change everything we thought we knew about the universe."

Rachel stared at the pamphlet, her brow furrowing in confusion. She reached out with a shaking hand, taking it from Reyes.

"What the hell is this?" she whispered, tracing a finger over the strange symbols.

Reyes leaned forward, her voice low and urgent. "That's what we need to find out. And I think it might be the key to bringing Mark back."

Rachel looked up, her eyes wide with a mix of disbelief and desperate hope. "What are you saying? That this... this thing has something to do with Mark?"

Reyes nodded, her expression grave. "I know it sounds insane, but hear me out. Strange things have been happening all over the world. Bizarre weather patterns, unexplained phenomena, people vanishing without a trace. And it all started around the time Mark disappeared."

She paused, gauging Rachel's reaction. The other woman sat perfectly still, her knuckles white as she gripped the pamphlet.

"I think..." Reyes swallowed, steeling herself for the words she was about to say. "I think Mark might have stumbled onto something big. Something that could have torn a hole in the fabric of reality itself."

Rachel shook her head, a hysterical laugh bubbling up from her throat. "A hole in reality? Jesus Christ, Reyes. You sound like one of those crackpot conspiracy theorists."

Reyes leaned back, running a hand through her hair. She couldn't blame Rachel for being skeptical. Hell, if someone had come to her with this theory a week ago, she would have laughed them out of the room.

"I know it sounds crazy," she said softly. "But the evidence is there. And if I'm right... if there's even a chance that this multiverse theory could lead us to Mark..."

She trailed off, letting the weight of her words sink in. For a long moment, the only sound was the ticking of the clock on the mantel.

Finally, Rachel spoke, her voice barely above a whisper. "If what you're saying is true... if Mark is lost somewhere in another universe... what do we do? How do we get him back?"

Reyes hesitated, the enormity of the situation crashing down on her. She'd been so focused on convincing Rachel, on finding answers, that she hadn't stopped to consider the consequences.

"I don't know," she admitted, her voice raw with emotion. "But we have to do something. We can't just sit back and let this happen."

She leaned forward, her eyes locking with Rachel's. "We need to decide whether to go to the authorities with this, or keep it to ourselves. Either way, there's no going back."

The silence stretched between them, heavy with the weight of the decision they faced. Both women lost in their own thoughts, grappling with the impossible choice before them.

Rachel's mind raced, torn between the desperate need for closure and the fear of what exposing the truth might bring. The thought of finally understanding what happened to Mark, of potentially bringing him home, filled her with a fierce longing. And yet...

"What if we're wrong?" she whispered, her voice cracking. "What if going public only leads to more pain, more questions without answers?" Her hands trembled as she clutched the worn fabric of the couch. "I don't know if I can handle losing him all over again."

Reyes leaned forward, her dark eyes intense. "I understand your fears, Rachel. But we can't ignore what's happening." Her words gained momentum, urgency seeping into every syllable. "The bizarre events, the inexplicable phenomena... it's not just us. It's happening all over the world."

She began to pace, her voice rising with each step. "Gravity fluctuations in Tokyo, temporal distortions in London, reports of people vanishing and reappearing in Rio." Reyes turned to face Rachel, her expression grave. "We're talking about the fabric of reality unraveling. If we do nothing, if we stay silent... the consequences could be catastrophic."

Rachel's heart raced, Reyes' words painting a terrifying picture of a world on the brink of chaos. She tried to imagine the global panic, the fear and confusion that would grip humanity if the truth came out. The weight of responsibility settled heavily on her shoulders.

"But what can we do?" Rachel asked, her voice barely above a whisper. "We're just two people, Reyes. How can we possibly hope to understand, let alone control, something of this magnitude?"

Reyes met her gaze, a flicker of determination in her eyes. "We start by finding answers. We track down experts, scientists who might be able to decipher the alien pamphlet. We pool our resources and our knowledge." She paused, her voice softening. "And we do it together, Rachel. For Mark. For everyone."

Rachel stood abruptly, her chair scraping against the hardwood floor. She paced the room, her mind reeling with the implications of Reyes' words. The weight of the world seemed to press down on her, suffocating her with its enormity.

She imagined cities in chaos, people running through the streets as the very fabric of reality tore apart. Governments collapsing, societies crumbling, and all the while, the alien pamphlet held the key to understanding it all. The thought made her stomach churn.

"Fuck, Reyes," Rachel muttered, running a hand through her hair. "This is... it's too much. How the hell are we supposed to handle this?"

Reyes watched her, her own expression tight with worry. "I know it's overwhelming, Rachel. But we can't afford to do nothing. The stakes are too high."

Rachel shook her head, a bitter laugh escaping her lips. "High stakes. That's putting it mildly." She paused, her gaze drifting to the photos of Mark that adorned the walls. Happier times, when the world made sense, and their biggest worries were paying the bills and arguing over whose turn it was to do the dishes.

A memory surfaced, unbidden. Mark, his eyes sparkling with mischief as he pulled her close, his lips brushing against her ear. "You and me, Rach," he whispered. "We're in this together. No matter what."

The memory was so vivid, so real, that for a moment, Rachel could almost feel the warmth of his embrace. She closed her eyes, letting the bittersweet nostalgia wash over her.

"I miss him so much," she said softly, her voice cracking. "He was my rock, Reyes. My partner in everything. And now..." She trailed off, unable to finish the thought.

Reyes crossed the room, laying a comforting hand on Rachel's shoulder. "I know, Rachel. And I can't imagine the pain you're going through. But Mark's work, his legacy... it's bigger than all of us now. We have to see it through, for his sake as much as ours."

THE HUSBAND

Rachel nodded, wiping away the tears that had begun to fall. She knew Reyes was right, as much as it hurt to admit it. They had a responsibility, not just to Mark, but to the world.

"Okay," she said, taking a deep breath. "Okay. We'll do this. We'll find the answers, whatever it takes."

Reyes leaned forward, her eyes intense. "There might be another way, Rachel. A third option we haven't considered."

Rachel looked up, her brow furrowed. "What do you mean?"

"What if we could find a way to control the effects of Mark's experiment? To reverse the damage it's causing?"

Rachel stared at her, stunned. "Is that even possible?"

Reyes shrugged. "I don't know. But think about it. If we could harness the power of the multiverse, bend it to our will... we might be able to fix this. To set things right."

Rachel shook her head, her mind reeling. "But how? We're talking about forces we barely understand, Reyes. The risks involved..."

"I know the risks," Reyes snapped, her frustration boiling over. "But what choice do we have? If we don't do something, the world as we know it could be torn apart. Is that what you want?"

"Of course not!" Rachel shot back, her own temper flaring. "But messing with the fabric of reality? Playing God? That's what got us into this mess in the first place!"

Their voices rose, overlapping in a heated exchange. Reyes paced the room, her hands gesturing wildly as she laid out her case. Rachel stood her ground, her arms crossed, her jaw set in a stubborn line.

"We have to try," Reyes insisted, her tone pleading. "For Mark's sake. For the sake of everything he believed in."

Rachel closed her eyes, her breath coming in short, sharp bursts. She knew Reyes was right, as much as it terrified her to admit it. They had to do something, even if it meant venturing into the unknown.

"Okay," she said at last, her voice barely above a whisper. "Okay. We'll try. But we need help, Reyes. We can't do this alone."

Reyes nodded, relief flooding her features. "Agreed. We need experts, people who can help us understand the science behind all of this. And that pamphlet... it might hold the key to everything."

Rachel sighed, the weight of the world settling on her shoulders. She knew the road ahead would be long and treacherous, fraught with dangers they could scarcely imagine. But they had no choice. They had to see it through, no matter the cost.

"So," she said, her voice steady despite the fear churning in her gut. "Where do we start?"

Reyes reached into her bag, pulling out the alien pamphlet. Its glossy surface caught the light, the strange symbols seeming to dance before their eyes. "We start with this," she said, her voice tight with determination. "We find someone who can translate it, someone who can tell us what the hell it means."

Rachel took the pamphlet, her fingers tracing the unfamiliar characters. "And then what?" she asked, her tone laced with uncertainty.

"Then we follow the trail, wherever it leads us." Reyes met Rachel's gaze, her eyes blazing with a fierce intensity. "We don't stop until we have answers, until we know how to fix this mess."

Rachel nodded, a flicker of hope igniting in her chest. It was a long shot, a desperate gamble, but it was all they had. "Let's do it," she said, her voice ringing with newfound resolve. "Let's find those answers."

They stood there for a moment, two women bound by a shared purpose, a shared grief. The road ahead was shrouded in mystery, but they would face it together, step by step, until the truth was finally revealed.

As the chapter drew to a close, Reyes and Rachel emerged from the house, their faces set with grim determination. They climbed into Reyes' car, the engine roaring to life as they sped off into the gathering darkness. The night sky loomed above them, vast and inscrutable, holding secrets they could only begin to fathom.

THE HUSBAND　　　　　　　　　　　　　　161

But they were ready, ready to face whatever challenges lay ahead. They had each other, and they had the knowledge that somewhere, somehow, the answers were waiting to be found. The journey had begun, and there was no turning back now.

Fuck the consequences, Reyes thought as she gripped the steering wheel, her knuckles turning white. They were going to see this through, no matter what. The world depended on it.

Detective Samantha Reyes paced in her cramped office, stepping over piles of scattered case files and empty coffee cups. The musty air clung to her like a damp towel. She scowled at the latest forensics report on the Jennings case. Still no damn leads. Her phone buzzed and she snatched it up. "Reyes."

"Detective, please, I need your help!" Rachel Jennings' strained voice crackled through the speaker. "I can't...I don't know what to do anymore."

Reyes sighed. Another sleepless night for the grieving widow. "Okay Rachel, let's meet. The usual spot."

Twenty minutes later, Reyes slid into a peeling vinyl booth at Moe's Diner. The air was thick with grease and desperation. Rachel was already there, slumped over a mug of coffee, stringy hair hanging in her gaunt face. She looked up at Reyes with bloodshot eyes.

"Tell me you found something, anything," Rachel pleaded, her voice cracking. Angry tears welled in her eyes.

Reyes shook her head as the waitress sloshed more bitter coffee into her chipped mug. "Nothing new. Trail's colder than a polar bear's ass."

Rachel slammed her fist on the sticky laminate table, drawing stares. "Dammit Samantha, it's been months! My husband is dead and no one seems to give a shit! I need answers!"

"You don't think I want to nail the bastard?" Reyes shot back, struggling to keep her own frustration in check. This case was a fucking enigma wrapped in a shit-stained mystery. She was busting her ass, but the leads kept evaporating like piss on a hot sidewalk.

Rachel buried her face in her hands, her shoulders shaking with silent sobs. Reyes shifted uncomfortably. Dealing with emotional wrecks wasn't exactly her forte. She awkwardly patted Rachel's arm. "Hey, I'm not giving up, alright? I'll find the son of a bitch, even if I have to turn over every rock in this godforsaken city myself."

Rachel sniffed and wiped her nose on her sleeve. "I just...I need to know why. Why Mark? What did he do to deserve this?"

Reyes wished she had an answer. She'd been asking herself the same damn question for months now. What was the motive? The more she dug, the more questions arose. But she couldn't let Rachel see her doubts. She had to be the rock, the hard-ass detective who always cracked the case. Even if she was grasping at straws.

"We'll figure it out," Reyes said with more confidence than she felt. "I've got a few more angles to work. This prick's bound to slip up sometime. And when he does, I'll nail his ass to the wall."

Rachel nodded, a faint spark of hope flickering in her deadened eyes. "Okay. Okay, yeah. Don't give up Samantha. Please. You're my only hope."

Reyes squeezed Rachel's hand, feeling the weight of her promise. She couldn't let her down. Even if it killed her, she'd find the bastard who murdered Mark Jennings. And she'd make him pay.

Reyes leaned back, her mind racing as she considered the evidence, or lack thereof, in the Jennings case. She took a deep breath and met Rachel's expectant gaze. "Listen, I've been thinking... What if we're looking at this all wrong? What if there's more to this than just a simple murder?"

Rachel furrowed her brow, confusion etched on her face. "What do you mean?"

"I know it sounds crazy, but hear me out," Reyes said, lowering her voice. "I've been researching this theory called the multiverse. It's the idea that there are multiple universes existing simultaneously, each with its own version of reality."

"Okay, but what does that have to do with Mark?" Rachel asked, skepticism evident in her tone.

Reyes hesitated, knowing how insane her next words would sound. "What if there are multiple versions of Mark out there? In different universes, living different lives?"

Rachel stared at her, eyes wide with disbelief. "You can't be serious."

"I know it's a long shot, but think about it," Reyes pressed on. "If there are other Marks out there, maybe one of them holds the key to solving this case. Maybe they know something we don't."

Rachel shook her head, a bitter laugh escaping her lips. "So, what? You're saying my husband is alive and well in some other universe? That's supposed to make me feel better?"

Reyes sighed, running a hand through her hair. "No, I'm not saying that. But if there's even a chance that we can find answers, don't you think we owe it to Mark to explore every possibility?"

Rachel fell silent, her gaze distant as she considered Reyes' words. A flicker of something - hope, perhaps - crossed her face, but it was gone as quickly as it appeared. "I don't know, Samantha. It all seems so...far-fetched."

Reyes nodded, understanding Rachel's reluctance. Hell, she could barely believe it herself. But she'd be damned if she let this case go cold. She had to keep pushing, keep digging, until she uncovered the truth.

Her mind drifted to the previous week, when she'd chased down a lead in the seedy underbelly of the city. She'd tracked a known associate of Mark's to a dingy bar, hoping to squeeze some information out of him. But the bastard had been tight-lipped, claiming he didn't know anything about Mark's whereabouts or the circumstances surrounding his death.

Reyes had left the bar frustrated and empty-handed, the stench of stale beer and cigarette smoke clinging to her clothes. She'd walked the streets for hours, her mind churning with unanswered questions and dead-end leads.

But she couldn't give up. Not now, not ever. She owed it to Rachel, to herself, to keep fighting until she brought Mark's killer to justice. Even if it meant chasing ghosts and grasping at straws, she'd follow every lead, no matter how outlandish or improbable.

Reyes snapped back to the present, her resolve hardening as she met Rachel's gaze once more. "Look, I know it's a long shot, but we have to try. We owe it to Mark to explore every avenue, no matter how crazy it seems."

Rachel sighed, her shoulders slumping in defeat. "Okay, fine. But how do we even begin to investigate something like this? It's not like we can just hop into another universe and start asking questions."

Reyes smiled, a glint of determination in her eyes. "Leave that to me. I've got a few tricks up my sleeve."

Rachel raised an eyebrow, a flicker of curiosity breaking through her despair. "What kind of tricks are we talking about here, Detective?"

Reyes leaned forward, her voice low and conspiratorial. "I've got a contact, a guy who knows a thing or two about quantum mechanics and theoretical physics. He's a bit of a mad scientist, but he might be able to help us track down any traces of Mark in the multiverse."

"You're not serious." Rachel shook her head, a humorless laugh escaping her lips. "This is insane. We can't just go messing around with the fabric of reality."

"You got a better idea?" Reyes challenged, her gaze unwavering. "Because from where I'm sitting, we're running out of options. If there's even a chance that some version of Mark is out there, don't you want to find him?"

Rachel hesitated, torn between the desperate desire for answers and the fear of what they might uncover. She thought of Mark, of the life they'd shared, the future they'd dreamed of building together. Could she really walk away from the possibility of seeing him again, even if it meant crossing the boundaries of time and space?

"Fuck it," she said at last, her resolve hardening. "Let's do it. Let's track down this scientist of yours and see what he has to say."

Reyes grinned, a spark of excitement igniting in her chest. "That's the spirit. We'll need to be careful, though. This kind of investigation could land me in some serious hot water with the department."

"I don't care," Rachel said fiercely. "I'm done playing by the rules. Mark deserves justice, and I'll do whatever it takes to get it."

Reyes nodded, a newfound respect for the woman across from her blooming in her heart. She'd underestimated Rachel, had assumed her grief would consume her, leaving her broken and helpless. But there was a strength in her, a determination that refused to be extinguished.

"Alright then," Reyes said, signaling the waitress for the check. "Let's get to work. We've got a multiverse to explore and a killer to catch."

As they paid their bill and gathered their things, Reyes couldn't help but feel a thrill of anticipation. They were embarking on a journey into the unknown, chasing a theory that defied the laws of physics and reason. But somehow, in that moment, anything seemed possible.

She glanced at Rachel, saw the steely glint in her eye, the set of her jaw. Together, they would unravel this mystery, would follow the threads of Mark's existence across the boundaries of reality itself.

And God help anyone who stood in their way.

The two women stepped out of the diner and into the frigid night air, their breath forming wispy clouds that dissipated into the darkness. The streetlights cast

The diner door swung open as Reyes and Rachel stepped out into the frigid night. Their breath crystallized in the air, dissipating like ghostly whispers. The cold bit at Reyes' exposed skin, but she barely noticed, her mind still reeling from their conversation.

"So, this is it then," Rachel said, hugging her coat tighter. "We're really doing this? Chasing down leads on fucking parallel universes to find my husband?"

Reyes met her gaze, seeing the raw desperation in Rachel's eyes. "Looks that way. I know it sounds crazy as hell, but what other choice do we have at this point? If there's even a sliver of a chance..."

Rachel nodded curtly. "Right. Well, guess I'll leave you to it. Let me know if you need anything from my end." She turned to go, then paused. "And Reyes? Thanks. For everything."

"Don't mention it. We're in this shit together now."

They parted ways, Rachel's footsteps echoing down the empty street as Reyes watched her go. A sudden gust of wind sent trash skittering across the asphalt. Reyes stuffed her hands in her pockets and headed for her car, mind already racing ahead.

Back at the precinct, Reyes slumped into her chair and surveyed the chaos of her desk. She pushed aside a stack of paperwork and booted up her ancient desktop. As she waited for it to wheeze to life, she drummed her fingers on the scratched surface, a staccato beat to accompany her churning thoughts.

Alternate realities, doppelgängers, wormholes... This was some straight-up science fiction fuckery. But if it meant finding Mark Jennings, or at least getting Rachel some closure, then she'd chase down every batshit theory out there. Anything beat sitting on her ass waiting for leads that wouldn't come.

The computer finally sputtered awake. Reyes cracked her knuckles and leaned forward, ready to dive headfirst down the rabbit hole. Time to cash in every favor and rattle every cage until something shook loose. There had to be someone out there who knew about this weird shit - some fringe scientist or unhinged genius. If they existed, she'd damn well find them.

But first, coffee. It was going to be a long fucking night.

The door slammed behind Rachel as she stumbled into her darkened apartment, the silence broken only by the jangle of keys hitting the floor. She kicked off her shoes, not bothering to turn on the lights, and made her way to the bedroom by muscle memory alone.

Collapsing onto the unmade bed, Rachel stared at the ceiling, the events of the day playing on repeat in her mind. Reyes' wild theories, the possibility of multiple Marks out there somewhere... It was too much to process. She rolled onto her side and reached for the framed photo on the nightstand - their last vacation together, smiling faces against a backdrop of sun-drenched sand.

"Where are you, Mark?" she whispered, tracing his features with a trembling finger. "What the hell happened to you?"

Suddenly restless, Rachel pushed herself up and padded to the closet. She tugged a dusty box from the back corner and carried it to the bed, settling cross-legged on the rumpled comforter. Inside, a jumble of mementos - ticket stubs, love notes, a faded t-shirt that still smelled faintly of his cologne.

At the bottom, a stack of photos. Rachel sifted through them, memories washing over her in bittersweet waves. Birthdays, holidays, lazy Sundays tangled together on the couch. She paused at one taken just days before he vanished - Mark grinning at the camera, eyes

Reyes leaned back in her chair, the wheels creaking under her weight. Her eyes flicked between the computer screen and the cluttered corkboard on the wall, the faces of witnesses and suspects pinned haphazardly among a web of red string. She rubbed her temples, willing the pieces to fall into place.

Her phone buzzed. A text from Rachel: "No luck on the forums yet. You?"

Reyes sighed. "Nada. Gonna try a new angle. These witnesses are full of shit."

She grabbed her coat and headed out, the chilly air slicing through her thin blazer. The first witness, a twitchy guy with a nervous tic, lived in a rundown apartment complex on the edge of town. Reyes pounded on the door.

"NYPD, open up!"

The door cracked open, the chain still latched. "Whaddya want?"

"Cut the crap, Marvin. I know you were at the bar that night. Spill."

Marvin's eyes darted. "I don't know nothin.'"

Reyes rolled her eyes. "Sure, and I'm the Queen of England. You saw Mark, didn't you? Or...someone who looked like him."

A flicker of recognition. Marvin glanced over his shoulder before leaning in, his voice dropping to a whisper.

"Okay, yeah, I saw a guy. Looked just like Mark. But it couldn't have been him, right? He was wearing different clothes, acting all weird."

Reyes' pulse quickened. "Where'd you see him?"

"Over by the old factory on the north side. But I'm tellin' ya, it wasn't Mark. This guy had a...a look in his eye. Like he wasn't all there, ya know?"

Reyes jotted down the location, her mind racing. Could it be a doppelganger from another timeline? Another version of Mark, bleeding through the cracks of the multiverse? She had to see for herself.

She fired off a text to Rachel: "Got a lead. Meet me at the old Jameson factory ASAP. Bring a flashlight...and maybe a gun."

Rachel stared at her phone, her heart pounding. After hours of combing through blurry photos and rambling conspiracy theories, finally a concrete lead. She grabbed her keys and dashed out the door, adrenaline coursing through her veins.

The factory loomed ahead, a crumbling behemoth silhouetted against the overcast sky. Rachel pulled up just as Reyes was climbing out of her car, a determined set to her jaw.

"What's the plan?" Rachel asked, trying to steady her shaking hands.

Reyes checked her gun, the click of the safety echoing in the eerie stillness. "We go in, we find this guy, and we get some goddamn answers. You ready?"

Rachel nodded, fear and anticipation mingling in her gut. Together they approached the rusted doors, the unknown waiting just on the

THE HUSBAND

other side. Reyes glanced at Rachel, a unspoken understanding passing between them. Then, with a deep breath, Reyes kicked the door open, and they stepped into the darkness.

The interior of the factory was a labyrinth of shadows and decay, the air thick with the stench of neglect. Reyes led the way, her flashlight cutting through the gloom, casting eerie shadows on the crumbling walls. Rachel followed close behind, her own light sweeping the corners, searching for any sign of movement.

"This place gives me the creeps," Rachel muttered, her voice echoing in the cavernous space. "You sure this is where your lead pointed?"

Reyes nodded, her eyes narrowed in concentration. "Positive. My source said they spotted someone matching Mark's description lurking around here. If there's even a chance it's him, or some version of him, we have to check it out."

They pressed on, navigating the twisted corridors and rusted machinery. The silence was oppressive, broken only by the crunch of their footsteps and the occasional skittering of unseen creatures in the shadows.

Rachel's mind raced as they walked, haunted by the memories of her lost husband. "What if...what if it really is him, Sam? What if we find him, and he's not the Mark I knew? What then?"

Reyes paused, turning to face her. "Then we deal with it. We find out what he knows, and we go from there. But Rachel, you have to be prepared for the possibility that this isn't going to be the reunion you're hoping for."

Rachel swallowed hard, nodding. "I know. But I have to try. I have to know the truth, even if it breaks me."

Reyes placed a comforting hand on her shoulder, her eyes softening. "I'm with you, every step of the way. We're in this together, no matter what we find."

They continued their journey, the bond between them growing stronger with each obstacle they faced. The factory seemed to go on forever, a never-ending maze of rusted metal and deep shadows.

Just as Rachel was about to suggest they turn back, Reyes held up a hand, her body tensing. "Did you hear that?" she whispered, her eyes scanning the darkness ahead.

Rachel strained her ears, her heart pounding. There, just on the edge of hearing, was the faint sound of footsteps, echoing from somewhere deep within the factory. The two women exchanged a glance, their grips tightening on their flashlights.

"Stay close," Reyes murmured, edging forward. "And be ready for anything."

They crept towards the sound, every nerve on high alert. The footsteps grew louder, the echoes bouncing off the walls, making it impossible to pinpoint their origin. Reyes and Rachel moved as one, their breath shallow, their eyes wide.

Suddenly, a figure stepped out of the shadows, silhouetted against the faint light filtering through a grimy window. Rachel's heart stopped, her flashlight beam illuminating a face she never thought she'd see again.

"Mark?" she breathed, her voice trembling. "Is it really you?"

The figure stared back at them, his expression unreadable. Reyes kept her gun trained on him, her finger hovering over the trigger. The tension in the air was palpable, the weight of unanswered questions hanging between them.

And then, the figure spoke, his voice achingly familiar yet tinged with an otherworldly echo. "Hello, Rachel. I've been waiting for you."

Rachel felt her breath catch in her throat, her mind reeling. Mark, or whatever version of him stood before them, took a step forward, his movements fluid and unnatural.

"What the fuck is going on?" Reyes hissed, her gun unwavering. "How are you here? How are you alive?"

Mark's lips curled into a smile that sent shivers down Rachel's spine. "I'm not the Mark you knew," he said, his voice resonating in the empty space. "I'm something more. Something beyond your understanding."

Rachel's heart raced, a mix of hope and terror coursing through her veins. "What do you mean? What happened to you?"

"I've seen things, Rachel," Mark continued, his eyes gleaming in the darkness. "I've traveled to places you can't even imagine. And I've come back, changed. Evolved."

Reyes glanced at Rachel, her brow furrowed. "This is some seriously fucked up shit," she muttered, her finger tightening on the trigger. "We need answers, now."

Mark spread his hands, his smile widening. "I have all the answers you seek," he said, his voice echoing off the walls. "But are you ready to hear them? Are you prepared to confront the truth, no matter how terrifying it might be?"

Rachel swallowed hard, her mind racing. She thought of all the sleepless nights, the endless hours spent searching for the man she loved. And now, here he was, standing before her, changed in ways she couldn't begin to comprehend.

"I'm ready," she said, her voice steady despite the fear coursing through her. "Whatever it is, whatever you've become, I need to know."

Reyes nodded, her jaw clenched. "Start talking," she growled, her gun still trained on Mark's chest. "And don't even think about trying anything funny."

Mark's laughter filled the air, a sound that sent chills down their spines. "Oh, detectives," he said, his eyes glinting with an otherworldly light. "You have no idea what you've stumbled into. But by all means, let me enlighten you."

And with that, he began to speak, his words painting a picture of a reality beyond their wildest imaginings, a truth that would shatter everything they thought they knew. Rachel and Reyes listened, their hearts pounding, their minds struggling to keep up, as they stepped further into the unknown, ready to confront the mysteries that had haunted them for so long.

The sense of impending revelation hung heavy in the air, the weight of the truth pressing down on them. And as Mark's words washed over them, they knew that nothing would ever be the same again.

Detective Samantha Reyes sat hunched over a corner table in the dimly lit Cuppa Joe's Café, an untouched mug of coffee growing cold beside her. The glow of her laptop screen reflected off the lenses of her glasses as she scrolled through the daily deluge of crackpot emails.

"Another sighting of Bigfoot, alien abduction story, missing time...Christ, when did I become the go-to girl for every tin foil hat wearing loon on the internet?" she muttered under her breath.

Her phone buzzed and lit up with yet another email notification. Reyes rolled her eyes and shoved the phone back in her jacket pocket.

"Guess I'm the X-Files hotline now," she scoffed, taking a swig of the burnt, bitter coffee and grimacing. "Just call me Agent Scully."

She turned back to the glowing screen, resigned to sifting through the endless stream of dead ends and delusions for any scrap of something real. Any lead that could blow this case wide open and vindicate her growing obsession with these so-called "quantum anomalies."

Her tired eyes scanned the subject lines:

"Vanished Into Thin Air - Quantum Kidnapping?"

"Doppelgänger Sighting - Glitch in the Matrix!"

"Am I Going Crazy? Unexplained Missing Time"

Reyes leaned back and rubbed her temples. She was definitely going to need something stronger than coffee to get through this.

Across town, Rachel Jennings strode through the doors of the Pineview Community Center, a warm smile already in place to greet the regulars milling about the front desk and cramped hallways. She returned their waves and "hello"s as she wove her way to the small meeting room in the back, the one with the faded yellow paint and stained grey carpet.

Rachel arranged the mismatched folding chairs in a circle, lining them up with care. She adjusted the "Quantum Anomalies Support Group" sign on the door, making sure it was positioned just right.

Taking a deep breath, Rachel centered herself, preparing to be fully present for whoever walked through that door today needing support, needing to be heard and believed when the world kept telling them they were crazy.

She knew that feeling all too well. The grief, the confusion, the desperate need for answers. It's what had brought her here, to this room and this circle of chairs, week after week.

Rachel took a seat and waited for the members to arrive, absently twisting the silver ring on her right hand - the one her sister Amber had given her for her birthday last year, before she vanished into thin air right in front of Rachel's eyes.

Quantum anomaly, the email groups called it. A glitch in reality. Rachel didn't know what to call it. All she knew was her sister was gone, and she was left behind to pick up the pieces. To find the truth.

The sound of approaching footsteps pulled Rachel from her reverie. She straightened up, readying herself. The first members were arriving, each carrying their own stories of loss and unanswered questions.

It was time to begin.

As the group settled into their seats, Rachel noticed a new face among the regulars. A woman in her mid-thirties with haunted eyes and a trembling lower lip. Rachel offered her a gentle smile of welcome.

"We have a new member joining us today," Rachel began, her voice soft but steady. "Would you like to introduce yourself and share what brings you here?"

The woman took a shaky breath, her hands clasped tightly in her lap. "My name is Lisa," she said, her voice barely above a whisper. "And my husband... he's gone. Vanished into thin air right in front of me."

Her words hung heavy in the room, a familiar refrain. Rachel leaned forward, her elbows on her knees, giving Lisa her full attention.

"It was our anniversary," Lisa continued, a single tear sliding down her cheek. "We were walking in the park, and he was holding my hand, and then... he wasn't. He was just gone. No flash of light, no sound. Just gone."

Rachel felt a pang in her chest, the story hitting close to home. She reached out and placed a hand on Lisa's knee, a gentle touch of comfort.

"I believe you, Lisa," she said, her tone unwavering. "You're not alone. We've all experienced something similar here. Something that defies explanation."

Lisa met Rachel's gaze, a flicker of hope in her eyes. "I've tried to tell people, but they look at me like I'm crazy. Like I'm making it up."

"You're not crazy," Rachel assured her. "And you're not making it up. The world just isn't ready to accept what's happening. But we are. We're here for you."

As the group continued to share and support one another, Rachel felt a sense of purpose settle over her. This was why she kept coming back, week after week. To help others navigate the uncharted waters of grief and uncertainty. To find strength in numbers and a shared mission.

Back at the café, Reyes was just draining the last of her coffee when a shadow fell across her table. She looked up to see a young man, early twenties, with a mop of unruly dark hair and wide, frightened eyes.

"Detective Reyes?" he asked, his voice trembling slightly. "I need to report a crime. Or... or something. I don't know what it was."

Reyes gestured for him to take a seat, pulling out her notebook and pen. "Alright, start from the beginning. What's your name?"

THE HUSBAND

"Ethan. Ethan Markham." He sat down heavily, his leg bouncing with nervous energy. "I saw... I saw myself. Another me. A doppelgänger."

Reyes fought the urge to sigh, keeping her expression neutral. Another one. They just kept coming out of the woodwork.

"Okay, Ethan. Tell me exactly what happened. Where were you, what were you doing?"

"I was at the library, studying for finals. I got up to grab a book from the stacks, and there he was. Me. Wearing the same clothes, holding the same book. He looked right at me, and then... he was gone. Blinked out of existence."

Reyes jotted down notes, her pen scratching against the paper. Studying at the library. Doppelgänger wearing the same clothes. Disappeared in an instant.

"And you're sure it wasn't just a trick of the light? A reflection, maybe?" she asked, knowing full well what his answer would be.

"No, it wasn't a reflection. It was me. Another me." Ethan's voice was insistent, his hands gripping the edge of the table. "I know how it sounds, but I swear I'm not making this up."

Reyes looked at him, taking in the fear and confusion etched across his face. The same fear and confusion she saw in the mirror every morning.

"I believe you, Ethan," she said, the words feeling heavy on her tongue. "I'll look into it. See if there have been any other reports of... doppelgängers."

Ethan sagged in relief, a shaky breath escaping his lips. "Thank you, Detective. I thought I was losing my mind."

As he left the café, Reyes stared down at her notes, a headache blooming behind her eyes. Quantum anomalies, glitches in reality, and now doppelgängers. When had her life turned into a science fiction novel?

She rubbed at her temples, trying to massage away the tension. She needed to talk to Rachel. Needed to compare notes and theories. Because as much as she hated to admit it, this was starting to feel bigger than both of them.

With a sigh, Reyes gathered up her things and headed for the door, steeling herself for another day of chasing the impossible. Another day in the twilight zone that had become her reality.

The diner buzzed with the lunchtime rush, a cacophony of clattering dishes and indistinct chatter. Rachel slid into the booth across from Reyes, her eyes widening as she took in the detective's haggard appearance.

"Damn, Sam. You look like hell."

Reyes snorted, pushing a wayward strand of hair from her face. "Feel like it too. This quantum bullshit is going to be the death of me."

Rachel's lips quirked in a wry smile. "Tell me about it. I had a guy in group today who swears he's been living the same day over and over again. Like some twisted version of Groundhog Day."

"At least he's not seeing double." Reyes leaned back, the vinyl seat creaking beneath her. "Had a kid come up to me at the café, freaking out about seeing his own doppelgänger."

"Seriously?" Rachel's brows shot up. "That's a new one."

"Right? As if the disappearances and glitches weren't enough, now we've got evil twins running around."

The waitress appeared, setting down their usual orders with a flourish. Reyes wrapped her hands around her coffee mug, relishing the warmth seeping into her palms.

"You know," she said, her voice low, "I'm starting to wonder if we're in over our heads here. I mean, quantum physics? Alternate realities? It's a bit above my pay grade."

Rachel shrugged, spearing a piece of lettuce with her fork. "Maybe. But who else is going to investigate this stuff? The FBI? They'd laugh us out of the building."

"True." Reyes took a sip of her coffee, wincing as it scalded her tongue. "But sometimes I feel like I'm losing my grip on reality. Like the other day, I swear I saw a car just... glitch out of existence. One second it was there, the next, poof. Gone."

"I know what you mean." Rachel's voice was soft, her eyes distant. "Last week, I was walking home from the community center, and I could have sworn the street signs changed. Just for a second, but it was like I was in a different neighborhood entirely."

They fell silent, each lost in their own thoughts. The absurdity of their situation hung between them, a shared secret they couldn't quite bring themselves to laugh about.

"We're not crazy, right?" Reyes asked, hating the tremor in her voice.

Rachel reached across the table, squeezing her hand. "No, we're not. But maybe the world is."

Reyes huffed out a laugh, the tension in her shoulders easing slightly. "Well, at least we've got each other. The dynamic duo of weird-ass phenomena."

"Damn straight." Rachel grinned, raising her glass in a mock toast. "To the X-Files hotline and the quantum queen. May we never run out of bizarro cases to solve."

Reyes clinked her mug against Rachel's glass, a smile tugging at the corners of her mouth. For a moment, the weight of the impossible felt a little lighter, a shared burden between friends.

But as they finished their lunch and parted ways, Reyes couldn't shake the feeling that something big was coming. Something that would test the limits of their sanity and their faith in the world as they knew it.

She just hoped they'd be ready for it when it did.

As they part ways, Reyes heads to a local library where she's scheduled to speak at a small gathering of anomaly enthusiasts. She reluctantly takes the podium, delivering a speech that balances skepticism with an open mind.

"I know you're all here because you've experienced something you can't explain," Reyes begins, her voice carrying across the hushed room. "I've been there too. Hell, I'm still there most days." She scans the faces in the crowd, seeing a mix of desperation and hope in their eyes.

"But here's the thing," she continues, leaning forward on the podium. "Just because we can't explain it doesn't mean there isn't an explanation. It's our job to keep looking, keep asking questions, even when the world tells us we're crazy."

She pauses, letting her words sink in. "I'm not here to tell you that aliens are real or that we're living in a simulation. I'm here to tell you that it's okay to not have all the answers. It's okay to be scared and confused and angry. But it's not okay to give up."

Reyes steps back from the podium, her heart pounding in her chest. She's not used to baring her soul like this, but something about this group makes her feel like she's among kindred spirits.

Meanwhile, Rachel's support group session continues, with members discussing coping mechanisms and sharing stories of hope and resilience. Rachel encourages them to find strength in each other, fostering a sense of community.

"I know it feels like the world is falling apart," Rachel says softly, looking around the circle of faces. "But we're still here. We're still fighting. And we have each other."

She takes a deep breath, feeling the weight of her own grief pressing down on her chest. "When my husband disappeared, I thought I'd never be able to move on. But coming here, talking to all of you... it's shown me that I'm not alone. That we're not alone."

A murmur of agreement ripples through the group, and Rachel feels a surge of pride. These people have been through hell, but they're still standing. Still hoping.

"We may not have all the answers," she continues, echoing Reyes' words from across town. "But we have each other. And that's a pretty damn powerful thing."

As the session winds down, Rachel watches the members of the group hug each other goodbye, exchanging phone numbers and promises to check in. She knows that the road ahead won't be easy, but for the first time in a long time, she feels like she's not walking it alone.

Reyes scans the audience, a sea of eager faces staring back at her. She takes a deep breath, steeling herself for the onslaught of questions.

A hand shoots up, and she nods at the man. "Yes, you there in the blue shirt."

"Do you think the government is behind these anomalies?" he asks, his eyes wide with conspiracy.

Reyes barely suppresses a snort. "I think if the government was capable of manipulating reality, they'd have better things to do than make people's socks disappear."

A ripple of laughter goes through the crowd, and she feels herself relax slightly. Another hand rises, this time from a woman in the front row.

"Have you ever experienced an anomaly yourself?" she asks, her voice trembling slightly.

Reyes pauses, considering her words carefully. "I've seen things I can't explain," she says finally. "Things that don't make sense according to the laws of physics as we understand them. But I try not to jump to conclusions. I'm here to investigate, not to speculate."

The questions keep coming, ranging from the plausible to the downright absurd. Reyes fields them all with a mix of humor and seriousness, trying to walk the fine line between skepticism and open-mindedness.

As the Q&A session draws to a close, Reyes feels a strange sense of accomplishment. She may not have all the answers, but at least she's asking the right questions.

Rachel sits alone in the empty community center, the chairs still arranged in a circle around her. She looks around the room, taking in the faded posters on the walls, the scuffed linoleum floor.

A year ago, she never would have imagined herself here. Leading a support group, helping others navigate the same uncharted waters she found herself in.

But then again, a year ago she never would have imagined her husband vanishing into thin air, leaving her with nothing but questions and a gaping hole in her heart.

She thinks back to those early days, the numbness giving way to a raw, aching grief that threatened to consume her. The sleepless nights spent staring at the ceiling, replaying their last conversation in her mind.

But slowly, painfully, she had started to heal. And a big part of that healing had come from this room, from the people who gathered here each week to share their stories and their strength.

Rachel knows she'll never stop searching for answers, never stop hoping for a miracle. But she also knows that she's not alone in this fight.

She takes a deep breath, feeling the weight of the past year settling on her shoulders. It's a heavy burden, but one she knows she's strong enough to carry.

With a final glance around the room, Rachel stands up and flicks off the lights. Tomorrow is another day, another chance to keep moving forward. And she'll be ready for whatever it brings.

The key jingles in the lock as Reyes pushes open her apartment door, the familiar scent of stale coffee and old paperwork greeting her like an old friend. She drops her bag on the floor with a heavy thud, kicking off her shoes and padding into the kitchen.

She grabs a beer from the fridge, popping the cap with a practiced twist of her wrist. The cold liquid soothes her throat as she takes a long swig, leaning against the counter and closing her eyes.

Her mind drifts back to the library, to the faces of the people who had come to hear her speak. Some had looked at her with skepticism, others with a desperate kind of hope. But all of them had been searching for something, just like her.

Reyes pulls out her notebook, flipping through the pages of scribbled notes and hastily sketched diagrams. She's been chasing these anomalies for months now, trying to make sense of the impossible. But the more she learns, the more questions she has.

She traces her finger over a particularly perplexing entry, a report of a man who claimed to have seen his own doppelganger walking down the street. It's the kind of thing that would have made her laugh a year ago, but now...

Her phone buzzes, jolting her out of her thoughts. She glances at the screen, seeing a text from Rachel.

"Another day, another mystery. When did our lives become an episode of the Twilight Zone?"

Reyes snorts, typing back a reply. "At least we're not alone in this crazy. Imagine trying to explain this shit to a normal person."

She hits send, tossing her phone onto the couch and taking another swig of her beer. The exhaustion is catching up with her now, weighing down her limbs like lead.

But even as her eyes drift shut, her mind is still racing. She can't shake the feeling that she's on the edge of something big, something that could change everything.

"Tomorrow," she mumbles to herself, setting the empty bottle on the coffee table. "Tomorrow, I'll figure it out."

And with that, she drifts off to sleep, her dreams filled with shadows and mysteries yet to be solved.

Mark Jennings weaved through the chaotic New York City streets, his mind a kaleidoscope of fragmented memories that didn't quite feel like his own. Yellow cabs screeched to a halt, narrowly avoiding collision as he darted across the crosswalk. The scent of hot dogs and pretzels from a nearby street vendor wafted through the air, mingling with exhaust fumes and the pungent odor of garbage awaiting pickup.

"Hey, watch it buddy!" a gruff voice yelled as Mark nearly collided with a burly construction worker.

Mark mumbled an apology, barely registering the interaction. He paused at the next intersection, the walk signal flashing an angry red hand. The city's energy pulsed around him, a living, breathing entity with secrets buried deep within its concrete veins. Whispers of alternate realities, of lives he'd never lived, brushed against his consciousness like an ethereal breeze.

"Get a grip, Jennings," he muttered under his breath. "You're losing it."

Across the ocean, in a quaint Parisian café, Rachel Jennings sat at a corner table, the Eiffel Tower looming just beyond the window. She took a sip of her espresso, the rich aroma and bold flavor a comforting constant in a world that felt increasingly unfamiliar. Her sketchbook lay open before her, the lines of the iconic tower taking shape beneath her skilled hand.

The buzz of her phone shattered her concentration. She glanced at the screen, expecting a message from her editor or perhaps her sister. Instead, a name she didn't recognize stared back at her: Mark Jennings.

"Who the hell...?" Rachel whispered, a frown creasing her brow.

She tapped the message, curiosity overriding caution. As she read the words, a chill raced down her spine, raising goosebumps on her skin despite the warm Parisian air.

"Rachel, it's Mark. I know this sounds crazy, but I think we're connected somehow, across different realities. I keep seeing flashes of your life, your world. Please, if you're getting this, we need to talk."

Rachel's heart pounded in her chest, the sketch of the Eiffel Tower forgotten. A sense of déjà vu washed over her, as if she'd lived this moment before in a dream half-remembered. She stared at the message, torn between the rational urge to dismiss it as a prank and the inexplicable pull towards this stranger named Mark.

"What the fuck is going on?" she breathed, her fingers trembling as she typed a response. "Who are you, and how do you know my name?"

The scent of cherry blossoms and the gentle babble of water enveloped Mark as he sat cross-legged by the koi pond, his eyes closed in meditation. Yet even in this serene Kyoto garden, he couldn't escape the nagging sensation that pulled at the edges of his mind—the presence of other Marks, their lives bleeding into his own.

"Focus, damn it," he muttered, trying to center himself. But the harder he tried, the more their consciousnesses seemed to brush against his, like whispers in a crowded room.

Suddenly, his eyes snapped open, his heart racing. He'd seen flashes of unfamiliar cities, caught snatches of conversations he'd never had. It was as if the boundaries of his reality were stretching thin, allowing glimpses of the other Marks to seep through.

"What the hell is happening to me?" he wondered aloud, his voice barely louder than the rustle of leaves in the breeze.

He stared at the koi swimming lazily in the pond, their scales glinting in the dappled sunlight. For a moment, he envied their simplicity, their existence untouched by the chaos of multiple realities colliding.

Mark took a deep breath, trying to ground himself in the present. He focused on the feel of the cool grass beneath his hands, the distant chime of a temple bell. But even as he sat there, he could feel the pull of the other Marks growing stronger, their lives tangling with his own in ways he couldn't begin to unravel.

"Shit," he breathed, running a hand through his hair. "I need answers."

With a sigh, he pushed himself to his feet, his mind already racing with questions. He knew he couldn't ignore this any longer—he had to find a way to understand what was happening, to make sense of the fragments of lives that haunted his every waking moment.

As he strode out of the garden, the scent of cherry blossoms fading behind him, Mark steeled himself for the journey ahead. He didn't know where it would lead him, but he knew one thing for certain: he wouldn't stop until he uncovered the truth behind the other Marks and the strange, impossible connection they shared.

Detective Samantha Reyes sprinted down the gritty London alley, her heart pounding in her chest. The suspect was just ahead, his silhouette barely visible in the dim light. She'd been on his tail for weeks, ever since the first reports of a man who looked uncannily like Mark Jennings started surfacing.

"Stop! Police!" she shouted, her voice echoing off the damp brick walls.

But the suspect didn't slow down. If anything, he seemed to move faster, his footsteps echoing like gunshots in the narrow alley.

Reyes gritted her teeth and pushed herself harder, her lungs burning with the effort. She couldn't let him get away, not when she was so close to finally getting some answers.

As she rounded the corner, she saw him up ahead, his back pressed against a dead end. Triumph surged through her veins—she had him cornered.

"Don't move," she warned, her hand hovering over her holster. "Turn around slowly, hands where I can see them."

The suspect obliged, his movements hesitant. As he turned to face her, Reyes felt her breath catch in her throat. It was Mark Jennings—or at least, someone who looked identical to him.

"What the fuck?" she muttered under her breath.

But before she could say anything else, the man vanished into thin air, leaving behind only a faint shimmer, like heat rising from asphalt on a summer day.

Reyes blinked, her mind struggling to process what she'd just seen. She took a step forward, her hand outstretched, half-expecting to feel the solid warmth of the man's body. But there was nothing there—just empty air and the faint scent of ozone.

"Goddamn it," she swore, holstering her gun with a frustrated sigh.

She stood there for a long moment, staring at the spot where the man had disappeared. Her mind raced with questions—who was he, how had he vanished like that, and what the hell did it all mean?

But one thing was clear: this case was far from over. And Samantha Reyes wouldn't rest until she uncovered the truth, no matter how impossible it seemed.

Neon colors danced across Rachel's face as she navigated the bustling streets of Neo Tokyo, her holographic map flickering before her eyes. The city was a dizzying labyrinth of towering skyscrapers and pulsing lights, but Rachel moved through it with purpose, her mind fixed on the task at hand.

Suddenly, a flash of movement caught her eye. She turned, her gaze drawn to the reflective surface of a shop window. There, staring back at her, was a man who looked eerily like Mark.

"What the hell?" Rachel breathed, her heart pounding in her chest.

She blinked, and the image was gone, replaced by her own startled reflection. Rachel shook her head, trying to clear the cobwebs from her mind. It couldn't have been Mark—he was a world away, lost in his own reality.

But the nagging sense of familiarity wouldn't leave her. She stepped closer to the window, her fingers brushing against the cool glass. For a moment, she swore she could feel the warmth of Mark's presence, as if he were standing just on the other side.

"Get it together, Rach," she muttered, turning away from the window and back to the neon-drenched streets. "You're losing it."

But as she walked away, she couldn't shake the feeling that something was off—that the boundaries between realities were beginning to blur in ways she couldn't even begin to understand.

The sun beat down mercilessly on the dusty streets of Nowhere, Texas, as Detective Samantha Reyes stepped out of her car. The heat was oppressive, but Reyes barely noticed—her mind was too focused on the case at hand.

She'd gotten a call from the local sheriff about a possible lead in the Jennings case. A witness had come forward, claiming to have seen not one, but three Mark Jennings arguing in the desert just outside of town.

It was a wild story, but Reyes couldn't afford to dismiss it out of hand. She'd seen too much in her line of work to rule anything out—even the impossible.

She made her way to the sheriff's office, her boots kicking up clouds of dust with every step. Inside, the air was thick with the stench of stale coffee and sweat.

"Detective Reyes?" a grizzled man in a cowboy hat asked, rising from behind his desk.

"That's me," Reyes said, shaking his hand firmly. "I hear you've got a witness for me."

The sheriff nodded, gesturing to a scrawny man slouched in a chair across the room. "That's him. Name's Billy Ray. Says he saw some weird shit out in the desert last night."

Reyes approached the man, her eyes narrowing as she took in his twitchy demeanor and bloodshot eyes. "Mr. Ray? I'm Detective Reyes. I understand you have some information about Mark Jennings."

Billy Ray looked up at her, his face pale and drawn. "I saw 'em," he said, his voice trembling. "Three of 'em, arguin' like they was gonna kill each other. But it wasn't just one Mark Jennings—it was three of 'em, all identical."

Reyes felt a chill run down her spine. "What do you mean, identical?"

"I mean they was the same damn person," Billy Ray said, his eyes wide with fear. "Same face, same clothes, same everything. Like some kinda fucked-up mirror trick."

Reyes leaned in closer, her heart pounding in her chest. "And then what happened?"

Billy Ray shook his head, his face pale. "They just...disappeared. Vanished into thin air, like they was never there at all."

Reyes straightened up, her mind racing. It was an impossible story—but somehow, she couldn't shake the feeling that it was true. That the boundaries between realities were beginning to break down, and that Mark Jennings was at the center of it all.

She thanked Billy Ray for his time and left the sheriff's office, her thoughts churning. She had a feeling that this case was about to take a turn for the bizarre—and that she was in for one hell of a ride.

The bitter cold nipped at Mark's exposed skin as he trudged through the deep snow, his breath forming icy clouds in the air. The towering evergreens cast long shadows across the pristine landscape, and the only sound was the crunch of his boots against the frozen ground.

He stopped in a small clearing and set to work building a fire, his hands moving with practiced efficiency. As the flames began to lick at the kindling, Mark felt a sudden warmth wash over him—a warmth that had nothing to do with the fire.

It was as if he could feel the presence of the other Marks, their consciousness brushing against his own like a whisper in the dark. He closed his eyes, letting the sensation wash over him, and for a moment, he swore he could see their faces flickering in the flames.

Rachel pushed her way through the crowded streets of Mumbai, the scent of spices and sizzling street food filling her nostrils. The market was a riot of color and sound, with vendors hawking their wares and customers haggling over prices.

She stopped at a stall piled high with vibrant spices, the owner eyeing her with a calculating gaze. "Finest saffron in all of India," he said, his voice smooth as silk. "For you, a special price."

Rachel arched an eyebrow, a smile playing at the corners of her mouth. "I'm sure you say that to all the girls," she quipped, picking up a small bag of the precious spice and inhaling deeply.

Suddenly, a familiar laugh caught her attention, and she spun around, her heart pounding in her chest. There, disappearing into the crowd, was a man who looked exactly like Mark.

Rachel dropped the saffron and pushed her way through the throng of people, her eyes scanning the sea of faces for any sign of him. But he was gone, vanished into the chaos of the market.

She stood there for a moment, her mind reeling. It couldn't be a coincidence—the man she had seen was Mark, or at least a version of him. And if he was here, in this reality...

Rachel took a deep breath, trying to calm her racing thoughts. She had a feeling that her world was about to be turned upside down—and that the answers she sought were closer than she ever could have imagined.

In a sleek Berlin office, Detective Samantha Reyes hunched over her desk, the glow of her computer screen casting an eerie light on her face. Files of the Jennings case lay scattered across the surface, a chaotic mosaic of leads and dead ends.

Reyes rubbed her temples, the beginnings of a headache throbbing behind her eyes. She had been chasing this case for months, ever since the first reports of a man named Mark Jennings appearing in multiple realities had surfaced.

Suddenly, her computer glitched, the screen flickering with a burst of static. Reyes leaned forward, her eyes widening as images of different Marks began to appear, each one wearing the same bewildered expression.

THE HUSBAND

"What the hell?" she muttered, her fingers flying across the keyboard as she tried to capture the images before they disappeared.

But as quickly as they had appeared, the images vanished, leaving Reyes staring at a blank screen. She sat back in her chair, her mind racing with possibilities.

"There's got to be a connection," she said to herself, her voice echoing in the empty office. "But what is it?"

As if in answer to her question, the world around her began to shimmer and dissolve, the walls of her office fading away like mist. Reyes blinked, her surroundings suddenly replaced by a surreal, dreamlike landscape.

She wasn't alone. Standing before her were multiple versions of Mark and Rachel, each one looking as confused as she felt.

"Where are we?" one of the Rachels asked, her voice trembling with fear.

"I don't know," Reyes replied, taking a step forward. "But I have a feeling we're about to find out."

The boundaries between their realities were dissolving, the very fabric of the multiverse unraveling before their eyes. Reyes exchanged a glance with the nearest Mark, a silent understanding passing between them.

They were in uncharted territory now, adrift in a sea of infinite possibilities. And as the landscape shifted and morphed around them, Reyes knew that the answers they sought were closer than ever before—but the journey to find them would be unlike anything they had ever experienced.

The landscape swirled and twisted, fragments of each reality colliding and merging into a kaleidoscope of chaos. Neon signs from Tokyo's streets crashed into the serene koi pond from Kyoto, while the Eiffel Tower loomed in the distance, its metal framework melting into the dusty streets of the Texas town.

"What the hell is happening?" Mark shouted over the roar of the shifting landscape, his voice barely audible amidst the cacophony of sounds.

Rachel stumbled, her hand reaching out to steady herself against a flickering hologram of a Mumbai market stall. "It's like our realities are collapsing in on each other!"

Reyes gritted her teeth, fighting to maintain her balance as the ground beneath her feet undulated like waves. "We need to find a way out of here before we lose ourselves completely!"

But even as the words left her mouth, Reyes felt her own sense of self beginning to fray at the edges. Memories from other lives, other realities, flickered through her mind like a film reel on fast-forward.

Mark closed his eyes, trying to focus on his own identity amidst the swirling confusion. But the more he tried to hold on, the more he felt himself slipping away, his consciousness merging with those of his other selves.

And then, through the chaos, he saw her. Rachel, her face a beacon of clarity in the maelstrom. He reached out, his fingers brushing against hers, and suddenly, everything snapped into focus.

For a brief, shining moment, they understood. The multiverse, in all its infinite complexity, lay bare before them. They saw the threads that connected them, the choices and chances that had brought them to this moment.

And they knew, with a certainty that transcended logic, that their story was far from over. That the convergence was only the beginning of a journey that would take them beyond the boundaries of what they had ever believed possible.

Mark tightened his grip on Rachel's hand, feeling the jolt of connection that anchored him to her, to himself. And as the landscape continued to shift and morph around them, he knew that whatever lay ahead, they would face it together.

The convergence reached its crescendo, a symphony of shattering realities and colliding destinies. Mark, Rachel, and Reyes stood at the epicenter, their minds exploding with a simultaneous epiphany that rewrote the very fabric of their beings.

In that instant, they saw everything. The intricate web of cause and effect that had brought them to this point, the infinite possibilities that branched out from every choice they had ever made. They saw the other versions of themselves, living out their lives in parallel universes, each one a reflection of what could have been.

And with that knowledge came a profound sense of peace, a realization that everything—the pain, the struggle, the moments of joy and despair—had been leading them to this moment.

The landscape around them shattered like a mirror, each shard reflecting a different reality. They fell through the cracks, plummeting into a void of infinite possibilities, their bodies and minds dissolving into pure consciousness.

Mark felt himself expanding, his awareness reaching out to encompass the entirety of the multiverse. He saw the birth and death of stars, the rise and fall of civilizations, the endless cycle of creation and destruction that played out on a cosmic scale.

And then, in a moment of perfect clarity, he found himself outside the universe, a silent observer watching the remnants of the convergence fade into nothingness.

From this vantage point, the struggles and triumphs of his individual life seemed insignificant, mere ripples in the vast ocean of existence. Yet he knew, with a certainty that went beyond words, that every ripple had its purpose, that every story, no matter how small, was an essential part of the grand narrative.

As he watched the last traces of the convergence disappear, Mark felt a deep sense of peace wash over him. The story was far from over, he knew. There were still mysteries to unravel, still choices to be made and chances to be taken.

But for now, in this moment of perfect stillness, he was content to simply be, to bask in the knowledge that he was a part of something greater than himself, a tiny but essential thread in the vast tapestry of the multiverse.

The camera lingers on Mark's face, his features illuminated by the soft glow of distant stars. His eyes, once filled with confusion and uncertainty, now shine with a newfound sense of purpose. A faint smile tugs at the corners of his lips, a smile that speaks of secrets learned and truths discovered.

He takes a deep breath, savoring the cool, crisp air that fills his lungs. Out here, in the vast expanse of the cosmos, everything seems clearer, sharper, more real than it ever did back on Earth. The petty concerns and trivial worries that once consumed him now seem laughably insignificant in the face of the endless possibilities that stretch out before him.

Mark's mind races with thoughts of the other versions of himself, scattered across the multiverse like so many pieces of a cosmic puzzle. He wonders what they're doing now, what choices they're making, what paths they're forging through the labyrinth of existence.

A part of him longs to reach out to them, to share the knowledge and insight he's gained. But he knows that each version of himself must find their own way, must navigate the twists and turns of their own unique journey.

As he stares out into the infinite expanse of the universe, Mark feels a sense of awe and wonder that borders on the spiritual. The mysteries of existence, once so daunting and impenetrable, now seem like an invitation, a challenge to be met head-on.

He knows that he'll never have all the answers, that the secrets of the multiverse will always remain just beyond his grasp. But that knowledge doesn't discourage him. If anything, it fills him with a renewed sense of purpose, a determination to keep pushing forward, to keep exploring the endless potential of the cosmos.

The stars twinkle and dance, their light a silent promise of the wonders that await. And Mark, his face aglow with the fire of discovery, knows that he's ready to meet them head-on, to embrace the infinite possibilities of the multiverse and all the adventures they hold.

The End.

Don't miss out!

Visit the website below and you can sign up to receive emails whenever Aaron Abilene publishes a new book. There's no charge and no obligation.

https://books2read.com/r/B-A-YOIP-MAAJF

BOOKS 2 READ

Connecting independent readers to independent writers.

Also by Aaron Abilene

505
505
505: Resurrection

Balls
Dead Awake
Before The Dead Awake
Dead Sleep
Bulletproof Balls

Carnival Game
Full Moon Howl
Donovan
Shades of Z

Codename
The Man in The Mini Van

Deadeye
Deadeye & Friends
Cowboys Vs Aliens

Ferris
Life in Prescott
Afterlife in Love
Tragic Heart

Island
Paradise Island
The Lost Island
The Lost Island 2
The Lost Island 3
The Island 2

Pandemic
Pandemic

Prototype
Prototype
The Compound

Slacker
Slacker 2
Slacker 3
Slacker: Dead Man Walkin'

Survivor Files
Survivor Files: Day 1
Survivor Files : Day 1 Part 2
Survivor Files : Day 2
Survivor Files : On The Run
Survivor Files : Day 3
Survivor Files : Day 4
Survivor Files : Day 5
Survivor Files : Day 6
Survivor Files : Day 7
Survivor Files : Day 8
Survivor Files : Day 9
Survivor Files : Day 10
Survivor Files : Day 11
Survivor Files : Day 12
Survivor Files : Day 13
Survivor Files : Day 14
Survivor Files : Day 15
Survivor Files : Day 16
Survivor Files : Day 17
Survivor Files : Day 18
Survivor Files : Day 19
Survivor Files : Day 20

Texas
Devil Child of Texas
A Vampire in Texas

The Author
Breaking Wind
Yellow Snow
Dragon Snatch
Golden Showers
Nether Region
Evil Empire

Thomas
Quarantine
Contagion
Eradication
Isolation
Immune
Pathogen
Bloodline
Decontaminated

TPD
Trailer Park Diaries
Trailer Park Diaries 2
Trailer Park Diaries 3

Virus
Raising Hell

Zombie Bride
Zombie Bride
Zombie Bride 2
Zombie Bride 3

Standalone
The Victims of Pinocchio
A Christmas Nightmare
Pain
Fat Jesus
A Zombie's Revenge
The Headhunter
Crash
Tranq
The Island
Dog
The Quiet Man
Joe Superhero
Feral
Good Guys
Romeo and Juliet and Zombies
The Gamer
Becoming Alpha
Dead West
Small Town Blues

Shades of Z: Redux
The Gift of Death
Killer Claus
Skarred
Home Sweet Home
Alligator Allan
10 Days
Army of The Dumbest Dead
Kid
The Cult of Stupid
9 Time Felon
Slater
Bad Review: Hannah Dies
Me Again
Maurice and Me
The Family Business
Lightning Rider : Better Days
Lazy Boyz
The Sheep
Wild
The Flood
Extinction
Good Intentions
Dark Magic
Sparkles The Vampire Clown
From The Future, Stuck in The Past
Rescue
Knock Knock
Creep
Honest John
Urbex
She's Psycho
Unfinished

Neighbors
Misery, Nevada
Vicious Cycle
Relive
Romeo and Juliet: True Love Conquers All
Dead Road
Florida Man
Hunting Sarah
The Great American Zombie Novel
Carnage
Marge 3 Toes
Random Acts of Stupidity
Born Killer
The Abducted
Whiteboy
Broken Man
Graham Hiney
Bridge
15
Paper Soldiers
Zartan
The Concepts of a Plan
The Firsts in Life
Vlad The Bad
The Husband
Giant Baby